D1648201

The

A c

r O

b a T

The

A c r O b a T

Edward J. Delaney

Turtle Point Press

Brooklyn, New York

Copyright © 2022 by Edward J. Delaney

All rights reserved. No part of this book may be reproduced or transmitted
in any form by any means, electronic or mechanical, including
photocopying, recording, or any information storage and retrieval system,
except as may be expressly permitted in writing from the publisher.

Requests for permission to make copies of any part of the work should be sent to:

Turtle Point Press, 208 Java Street, Fifth Floor, Brooklyn, New York 11222
info@turtlepointpress.com

Library of Congress Cataloging-in-Publication Data
Names: Delaney, Edward J., 1957- author.
Title: The acrobat / Edward J. Delaney.
Identifiers: LCCN 2022024342 (print)

Design by Keenan

Paperback ISBN: 978-1-885983-03-9
Ebook ISBN: 978-1-885983-06-0

Printed in the United States of America

First Edition

This is a work of imagination,
Inspired by a life

For Jenn, again.

Contents

Thus play I in one person many people,
And none connected. Sometimes I am king;
Then treason makes me wish myself a beggar,
And so I am. Then crushing penury
Persuades me I was better when a king.

Shakespeare,
Richard II

HE'S SOARING, FAR ABOVE the earth. Hung in the sun, swaddled in the deep blue firmament, feeling as if he can never fall. Gravity has granted him reprieve, and time has bated its flow, all just for him.

The Acrobat revels in sensation, bright lightness made of molecules binding with imagination. He savors the blade of horizon cutting around him, a somersaulting azimuth, orbiting him as planets orbit a bright and burning center.

He inhales a thin and bracing air. Yet his body feels overheated, and his pulse thumps away, even reclined on the leather fainting couch from which his mind makes its vaults and flips, now that the LSD has taken its fullest hold of him. Dr. Hartman sits in his chair, nearby, Virgil to his Dante. It's a warm Beverly Hills afternoon outside the windows. In this blind-darkened, air-conditioned hush, the Treatment has rendered a world in vivid and as-before-unseen hues.

He tumbles forth, nominally on this temperate day in 1959, corporeally on the couch, but spiritually across decades and places. The comfort of that fetal, ovoid tuck-and-roll is as familiar as cradling arms. He hasn't been in the air this way in decades, but as instantly he is tumbling again in the smoke-filled air of the Bristol Hippodrome in 1918, following a different arc under blue light. And now he's falling from his stilts amid the bumptious Coney Island crowds in 1922; the boardwalk rises up to slam him. But he passes through the boards as if through a dense fog; on the other side he sweeps out over the clear water, high in a perfect dive over the blue of the old swimming pool at the Santa Monica cottage, 1936, Randy and the assembled guests watching him from white chaise longues. The Acrobat gives this flight a well-practiced flourish, and now it's become the dive onto dusty ground, clad in a gray suit and silver necktie on a long road under endless sky. Hitch is behind the big VistaVision camera with the crew all around and lights brighter than the weak intrusion of the noonday sun over Bakersfield. And without truly landing in any of these places, but floating over them in an ether of memories both distant and close, he feels beneath him the soft cloud of upholstery, the doctor's workaday couch, the beginning and ending of all these daring, Icarian flights as the wax of his wings melts under the heat of his recollection. He is at home, in the sky, but now gravity has begun its downward pull.

Afterward, late afternoon after the hours of the session followed by the hours of slow return from the LSD, he needs to eat. Enervated, he enters a small sandwich shop off Wilshire. He could see, from the back seat of his Rolls-Royce as it passed, that the place was empty—perhaps no ringing endorsement of the food, but preferable to the stares he could not abide right now. He's still finding his legs from his leaps and trajectories.

The waitress, youngish, has eyes with no dreams in them. She takes no particular note of him and when his sandwich comes, he realizes the hunger has left him as quickly as it had come. He sits, and stares at the chicken sandwich, and knows he's nowhere near finished with his ruminant journey. He feels as if still unspooling from a long, tight binding. He nearly feels vertigo.

And can't stop drinking water. He downs a glass, and the waitress refills, and he drinks that down with long and slaking gulps.

The waitress, he realizes, is still standing before him.

"Is something wrong with your food?" she says, the tone laced with accusation. He can see her words floating in the air around her with the lightness of snowflakes. The dosage will yet take time to wear off.

"No, my dear, nothing's wrong at all."

"Well, you still have to pay for it, you know."

And herein, the endless conundrum of fame. Is she aware of who he is, he thinks, and his undeserved portrayal by the gossip columns as a miser? Or is this simply the way a small shop in a college neighborhood would think (even of a well-dressed man)? As in so many instances, he'll never be sure. He is the known man, laden with his own success, tethered to the earth with the fame he once thought would make everything right.

And he desperately needs more water.

Constellations

HIS MIND CONJURES A *world in which everyone is a star. A galaxy in which each human being stands out and each forms the greater beauty of creation. Everyone is cherished, and honored, and loved. Everyone is seen and elevated. Each person deserves the world's attention, and its respect. A world of performers, playing the roles they've been cast in. In this world, everyone is special by not being special. The queen of England is worthy, but no more so than a laborer in the field, who worthily plays the role with dignity and conviction. When everyone is a star, no one is found wanting. No one feels shame. No one suffers.*

All the world's a stage, as the Bard said, but that also means everyone dons a mask. You can't ever tell what's under it. Nor does it matter. We love and cherish the mask without knowing what's deeper. We can touch the movie screen with our hands and feel nothing. Inside the costumes may lie unheeded people with silent urges that don't follow any script. The script gives them direction, and purpose. The predestined nature of their roles and the limits of their freedom, determined by some unseen hand, keep them on a straight road. How can one feel shame when they simply recite the expected lines, and enact the expected motions?

Even the criminals are following the script that's been handed them. They serve their own purpose in the world, as good stories need heroes and villains; each person is an expression of a particular form of need, desperation, happiness, or aspiration. It's all accepted as the complexity of the world's very fabric.

But in this world in which we are all players, we likewise find no audience. Everyone is on the stage, so no one is in the seats. Each actor plays the part of one who listens and watches, but that really is no more than a feature of their performance. They only wait to speak again, pausing until the next cue.

But they're happy in their freedom from indecision. Very few of them agonize as to who they should be or how they should conduct their lives; everything is predetermined. No one suffers from their mistakes; all is how it should be.

But then there are those few lonely wanderers who have been left from such certainty. Somehow, they were missed. They seek their place, and they never feel quite situated. They feel the constriction of their assigned costumes and lines. They listen for their cues but don't hear anything, so they improvise and create. They feel miscast, untethered, hidden in the shadows at the stage's edge, unnoticed or sometimes noticed too much.

How can they be unhappy among all the happy faces? There are some small joys in seeing uncertainty looming ahead, as uncertainty is infused with possibility. In this world, this unscripted life of a few wayfarers can be terrifying, and exhilarating, and dangerous. They travel new roads, but silently: Everyone else, in their worlds, assumes these people are just fellow actors, and presume that what

8

they do is as scripted as their own comfortable sinecures.

1959

PASSION CANNOT BE FINESSED. Nor can it be reserved. Lust, even less so. All the careful ministrations, all the delicate repartee, all the small gestures, and then to a sweat-streaked bed where the field of play shows signs of battle and surrender. The cigarettes burning in ashtrays, clothing strewn across floors, a pair of martini glasses drying on the night table, the air humid and redolent, the first glow of sun hitting the treetops, the deep inhalations and pensive touches on new flesh. Kaleidoscopic, wheeling, dreamlike.

And then the quiet click of the door and the Acrobat is alone again, an aging man, savoring his vigor, swept up by sensation and risk. Another stranger, a friend for a night or maybe a few, then the hush, both immediate and extended, words not spoken and tales not told, and then the hunt beginning anew.

To dress in crisp shirts and razor-creased suits is to reenter civilization. Here is the finesse. A fresh shave, the spritz of cologne, the socked feet sliding into the calfskin caress of bespoke shoes. Exactly 281 millimeters in length and 107 millimeters in width for the left foot; the right 279 and 108. Asymmetrical, the way he can see his face is; he notes in the mirror the slightly lower-set right eye that makes the right side of his face the better one. And two features that should be obvious to all, but seem not to be. The first is the part of the hair on the "wrong" side, which is right for him. That came from the director von Sternberg on the set of *Blonde Venus*, who spat out in that guttural Viennese accent that the hair was all wrong. And it must have been, as that movie

9

seemed to raise his fortunes.

The second thing should be even more obvious; he has secretly wondered if it was the true ingredient to his appeal: that he only has one front tooth. He lost the other, the right central incisor, as a boy. On a long-ago winter's day, running across icy paving stones and losing his footing and slamming down face-first. The tooth, spat out onto the wet pavement; the blood, filling his mouth; the first thought, about how angry his father would be. For a long while afterward, he'd kept his mouth mostly quiet, though to be a working-class lad with a gap seemed quite normal. But then, the odd denouement: Over the next few years of puberty, as he filled out and his jaw came in, the teeth slowly drifted toward each other and the gap inexplicably closed itself. His imperfect smile somehow made itself perfect. Had the tooth not been lost, he imagines the result would have been a busy and overcrowded mouth not unlike his father's, that toothy Anglican overbite. The nine-millimeter difference, it seems, between a leading man and a character actor.

Many a man absent a front tooth might have been sure not to smile, but to become a smiling performer was, to him, like showing people exactly who you were and having them simply not notice. Later on, a little bit of covert dentistry ordered by the studio helped further; the dentist ground the Cyclopean tooth so the line matched the surrounding lateral incisors, leaving a cockeyed grin that aimed to please. Even as the film technology got better, and the screens larger, and the lenses sharper, no one seemed to pick up on something he felt was so patently obvious. Another of his secrets right out in plain sight.

Yet he's always been convincingly false, as actors always are. Made up and powdered down and blushed and dyed, so as to appear completely natural. Authentic on the screen, like a piece of wax fruit. The actresses were all magnificent. Shining, drool-inducing beauty, best left on the movie-house screen. And that's where he's different. He's the real item, disguised as wax fruit. The odd-toothed man, unrecognized as such. Well, all right, there was one: The producer Mack Sennett, still floating around Hollywood after the collapse of Keystone Studios, had approached him at a cocktail party and mumbled in his ear that he was in on the secret: "Three teeth where there should be four . . ." That Sennett saw it from a theater seat was impressive, but this was the man who'd once assembled the famous Bathing Beauties, so he knew what for. He gleaned the secret code that makes people feel he's just like them, even in his riches and glory.

The film he'll be shooting is of middling interest to him. Another piece of light fare that will earn him sizable money, and nothing more. Bob Hope turned down the role he'll be playing, which says everything. But he's come to be able to do these pictures nearly by rote. And, of course, he's negotiated an ownership stake, and a percentage of the gross. No fool, he.

He comes by the studio the day after New Year's, just to see what's going on. On Soundstage Eight, he watches Scotty McDonald, the head gaffer, setting up lights with his crew and sees a kindred spirit: a lot of jobs done, a level of excellence achieved, but no more fire under the cauldron about it all.

Scotty sees him and ambles over, the usual hint of mischief in his eyes.

"Boss," he says, "I was just telling the fellows that acting is what happens to good-looking guys who aren't good at anything useful."

"Lucky none of you fellows are good-looking, then."

Scotty smiles and says, "Who wrote that one for you?"

"I'm actually capable of independent thoughts, my dear man. And it's always been a problem."

The Acrobat watches one of Scotty's younger charges at the top of a ladder, adjusting the barn doors on a hanging light.

"Scotty, there was a time I lived like that, on ladders and stilts and wires, out there by myself. High in the sky."

"Did you get afraid or something?"

"Not afraid at all. Never had much chance to think about it, really." The Acrobat points to the young man. "I could still be up there. How about if I go up the ladder next?"

"No chance. The talent's not allowed to clamber. I'd lose my damned job."

"It feels odd to have my feet on the ground sometimes. No risk anymore. No excitement, at least of that sort."

"Boss, I've been married to the same woman forty years and have had this job about as long. No excitement can be a joy."

"There are certainly joys to which I might not have given their due."

"Seriously? Now, is that you, or a line from a show?"

"I actually admire what you have, Scotty."

"And I admire what you have," Scotty says, nodding toward a girl, apparently an extra, who is standing at the base of the ladder and hardly gaping at all.

Vanity and shame and preening and avoidance. His impulses, when he doesn't have a studio script to follow, so often seem oppositional and hard to master. When he's at home, stuck in the stasis of being "between projects," he feels his most vulnerable. He feels most anxious just before a picture goes into production. He has the house in Palm Springs, which helps when he can get there. But he's stayed here in Los Angeles as he engages in the Treatment.

So he is the man in his manor. Tight inside a box of locks forged to keep out the world.

He wanders, restless, from room to room. He's Citizen Grant in his hall of mirrors. Betsy had gotten a decorator who told them lots of mirrors "opens up the room with light." But now Betsy's gone, off to London and probably for good, and every time he turns his head he sees himself looking at himself.

The funny thing is, he always catches himself by surprise. As if he's seen a ghost. A strange sense of his father's face. Or maybe one of the characters he's occupied and then abandoned, so many that their names run together. Noah and Eugene and Dudley and Mortimer, whimsical names for whimsical men who evaporate in the moments after the final scene is shot, but now hover in the reflections in his empty house, as skeptical of him as he always was of them. He stands at a distance from many selves and wonders why they're looking at him like that. In the inversion of the mirror image, they all have their hair parted on the proper side.

But the women never show up in those mirrors. Women he's romanced and at times married, and each from whom he has parted, so many their names run together. Virginia, Phyllis, Barbara, Betsy, and any number of smaller interludes. Just when he thinks they might be looking over his shoulder, with some amused measure of disappointment or concern, they're nowhere to be found, specters who have vanished from his field of vision. That makes him wonder how much he'd ever cared, or they. Every marriage was meant to be permanent and ended up just as fleeting as another role he played. But he's seeing, as well, that he is seeking something none of them could provide, though he has no idea what that something would be.

The closets are filled with the suits, his version of a terra-cotta army. They are creased to such edges that his clothes-presser father would have nodded in approval. The Acrobat was imbued by his lineage to occupy the suit, like armor against the chaos of the world, like splints of thread and starch, to prop him up and give him shape. He is both all he should be, and none of it, when he cinches the knot of a silk tie to his throat; his other clothes (the tennis outfits, the swimsuits, the ascots and the cashmere sweaters and polo shirts) feel as much costumes as the harlequin he sometimes donned as a young performer. The suits are like most of his roles in these films of his: basically the same, with subtle alterations.

By the cavernous closet, there's a shelf with a purpose known only to him, and embarrassingly so. A few meaningless knickknacks fill the space, but he's always had his silent designs. His own small share of negative capability. This is where his Oscars are supposed to go, until they never come.

He's not thinking of the ones he lost after he was actually nominated. His roles in *Penny Serenade* and *None but the Lonely Heart* were there for all to see, and to judge, and were summarily found wanting. What he rues instead are all the roles he turned down, where, as he watches those pictures now, he still can only see himself. *Roman Holiday. The Big Sleep.* No one could rightly imagine him now as Joe Bradley or Philip Marlowe. But he'd had each of these men in his hand, and had let each slip away. He'd also narrowly missed being on some real failures, like *It's a Wonderful Life*. He'd wanted to be George Bailey, but ended up being happy enough when Jimmy Stewart took it, and the picture didn't earn out. But his heart sinks especially thinking back on *A Star Is Born*, which he'd first signed on for, then dropped out of. Judy Garland had been cast in what was to be her big comeback; at the same time, word of her drug problems had become alarming, and he worried the picture would be a disaster. It was not, as it turned out, and there'd never be a chance quite like that again.

Selznick, who was in a co-production deal with London Films, had begged him to do the Harry Lime role in *The Third Man*. "It's perfect for you," the great producer had said through the phone, in that nasal lisp of his that could make people underestimate him. "It will change everything in the way people see you." But the Acrobat froze up. He begged off, saying the production schedule in London and Vienna would clash with other commitments. But the reality was he was hesitant to take the leap: He'd worked so hard to be who he was, why did he want to be seen differently? The Acrobat chose *I Was a Male War Bride* instead, safe and lucrative comedic ground that nonetheless made him feel untrue to himself.

In came Orson Welles to be Harry Lime. Welles, who always played things in that weighty rumble. Welles's friend Joseph Cotten took the Holly Martins role. The Acrobat saw the picture, alone in a screening room on the MGM lot (arranged via Selznick mostly to rub his face in it), and saw what he could have been. He nearly groaned at some of the Welles scenes, too stentorian, too excruciatingly aware of the camera, and the Acrobat further groaned at the lost moments that could have been his. Welles didn't win the award, but didn't need to: He had his, from *Kane*, and besides, nobody seemed to like him these days anyway.

The problem with choosing a role is that it's like choosing a wife. It's filled with hopes for so much, often unrealistic hopes lit from the first sparks, and always such a tenuous choice. He's seen things go very badly. He's come to grief. And so he's withheld his love when he might have best been offering it. For every role he takes, there is What Might Have Been. And the same for every role he refused. He sees his shelf of knickknacks, as if a nursery of children never conceived, as grand as they might have come to be.

Between the work on the pictures, in these quieter junctures of life, he feels even more aloft. Sitting in his pajamas, watching television: What to make of all this parading across this stunted little monochrome screen? So small, and of so little consequence. From time to time, he'll come across one of his own pictures, playing on the late show or the midnight movie, and he'll feel duly diminished. Made into a tiny man inside a box. Not like the childhood days in the darkened Metropole with the great stars cast two stories high. He was a young boy and everything seemed outsized, but Fairbanks was Gulliver, and the audience Lilliputians; now, even his expensive Zenith Space Command 400 television in his expensive living room cannot match the inherent grandeur the pictures had in that seedy old barn on Ashley Road. The silvered light dancing in the cloud of smoke rising from the men's cigarettes, sacramental as incense.

Back through the door of the Psychiatric Institute of Beverly Hills, and the same anxiety as if waiting for the stage curtains to part. The hush of cheap carpets and the plain wood-paneled walls and nondescript furniture in a pricey suite in the heart of Beverly Hills. It's the antithesis of his luxe home, and those of his fellow clients here; the hair shirt of shag rugs and nubby brown sofas and forgettable art on the wall. The stripped-down, egoless room of the mind.

In his fugues of memory and perception, when the LSD has moved like a bay fog across his scarred consciousness, there is always the return to a singular moment, when his solitary journey began. The point of his sessions with Dr. Hartman is to go there, to live it again and from this place find the room for forgiveness. The drug is sometimes called truth serum, but the Acrobat sees it as sharpening the edges of truth as if on a whetstone. The pain of return is always awaiting him, a fresh shock of a long-ago moment, or a vision of what could have been, or what will be.

When he's finally settled on the chaise and the blinds have been drawn and the doctor's assistant has brought him the dose, the pill from the bottle labeled *Delysid* and *Sandoz Ltd., Basle,* his mind is still not peaceable. It will be an hour before the pill begins to take true effect, and another hour before the doctor takes his place beside the couch and begins to accompany him through another circle in the inferno, seeking new discovery and unearthing new pain from old wounds.

1920

THE FIRST THIN TRACE of landfall came first to the youngest, they of sharp eyes and fulminating expectations. The older people followed; they squinted and implored, "Where? Where is it?" The ship's engines thrummed, the deck buzzing heavy beneath his feet. The travelers hugged the bow's rail after five days of seeing only endless water, as if to get themselves that much closer to land.

Aboard the RMS *Olympic*, on this late-July morning of 1920. All of them out in a humid dawn, with the sun rising over the sea behind them and the bow cutting whorls of sea-tanged foam. Archie saw the first glint of low sun hitting some distant pane of New York City glass, a pinprick twinkle off the heights of a not-as-yet-visible skyscraper, like a plaintive lighthouse. Almost there, almost. Archibald Alec Leach, sixteen years old and deep in his apprenticeship in the acrobatic arts and sciences, couldn't help but gape. America was slowly revealing itself like an inked brushstroke added between sea and sky. He wanted to walk it like a tightrope.

Archie, one of a troupe of his own kind, boys from the common houses of common towns, about to embark on the "Raid of the Ungrateful Colonies," as Bob Pender, their employer, had referred to it when Americans were out of earshot. The raid was commencing and concluding in New York City, with scheduled forays into an interior as dark and mysterious as deepest Africa's: Missouri, Ohio, Iowa. The ship's guttural vibration only added to the butterflies churning in his own stomach.

"Archie, is your bag ready?" Pender growled from behind him, showing his own nervous state.

"Yes, sir, on my berth."

"Well, go down and get it. We'll be headed straight to the theater, so no place for delays."

Pender still treated him like a child, but Arch had grown immeasurably since the ship first cast its lines in Southampton and moved to open sea. That first morning, he'd stood near the bow, looking resolutely westward at the horizon and the endless ocean yet to traverse, while his fellow troupers stood at the stern, watching England recede into the mist. As the ship settled into its forward push and passengers began to settle themselves in for the journey, Arch stayed locked on what lay ahead. He was willing a new life for himself, different from the pain and privation of his own circumstances. Could one shed his unhappiness as one could push off into open sea? Clearly, he thought; clearly.

Almost immediately after the ship was underway, word had spread, as would an electric shock, that the great actors Douglas Fairbanks and Mary Pickford were on board. They were the brightest stars in that distant galaxy, Hollywood, and they were somewhere on this vessel. Arch had slept fitfully in his narrow berth that first night, livened by their rumored proximity. If he'd stood at either end of the long ship, he'd have still been within 882 feet of them, too close to make for peaceful slumber.

Somewhere in the small hours, when he began to imagine

18

dawn rising outside the windowless hutch of a cabin, Archie had made it his mission to find them.

The six boys who constituted the Pender Troupe's "male apprentice wing" were stuffed, for the duration, into one small third-class cabin. It was a room with tightly spaced bunks, a single lightbulb, and the incessant roaring vibration of the massive ship's engines laboring just beneath them. The eight girls in the troupe were likewise grouped in fours, with Mr. and Mrs. Pender themselves up in second class. Once Arch began to form a resolute plan, he had also determined he was not about to bring any of the others along on his expeditionary efforts. He'd earned his way onto this ship, and not by being a fool. From the moment at age eight when he'd stepped into the Bristol Hippodrome on a school field trip, to look at the electric lights, each egress from that grimy, sacred space was like stepping back out into an unyielding world. He'd immediately set himself to being part of it.

As the others slept, Arch put on his best white shirt and his father's second-best tie, and his one suit that was just at the edge of shabby but perhaps presentable enough. He left his room in a cat's silence and made his way up to find the places where he could breach the barriers meant to keep out his kind. He was aiming for the first-class sun deck.

On that second morning out of port, he waited until after breakfast time, not eating anything himself, and quietly found a high barrier separating his own ilk from the more lofty, at a place where no one was watching. He vaulted over easily. And now on a whim he walked the ship's rail, as he would on a tightrope, balancing in the wind and knowing a slip would send him plunging sixty feet down into the ocean, never to be heard of again. And the easy leap back onto the deck. Once over, he knew he could be that lofty lad. His legs had gotten him here and now his looks and his manner would allow him to stay.

On a wood-slatted bench facing the rail, and the vast ocean beyond, he waited. A summer morning, sure to bring out the gentry to stroll the deck. He savored the briny lilt of soft morning air, the spray's remnants rising out of the bow's insistent push through open sea. Somehow, even the air felt better in first class. For a moment, he considered getting up on the rail again, to show everyone who he was. But instead he gathered some patience. He wanted to make this day important.

And then he saw them. They were moving along the deck, easing through the parting crowd of admirers, making their own wake of turned heads and approving glances. Fairbanks and Pickford, in flesh and color and sound. He'd countenanced them endlessly on the monolithic screen of the theater, pristine in both silence and monochrome. But even scaled down to life-sized, they loomed over everything. Fairbanks was at least half a head shorter than Arch himself, who'd already reached six feet and two. Pickford, the giant of the screen, was plainly tiny. She seemed little more than five feet tall. Despite the warmth of the morning, she was wearing a mink stole over a light coat, and a wide hat against the open sky. Fairbanks wore a double-breasted blue suit and a straw boater. Arch studied every detail of Fairbanks until they got close enough to notice him.

Arch averted his gaze now, setting the lure. He'd learned this essential truth about stars: The only thing they hated more than being noticed was not being noticed. They approached stage left; past Arch was an assortment of shuffleboard cues and disks. He stood slowly, selecting a stick with studied intent. He sighted down its shaft as if to gauge its trueness, though he'd never played this game in his life. But he was demonstrating such focus! This was important to the performance. He could only sense their approach, but he timed the beats and then waited one beat longer. Then he looked up and they were right there.

"Are you a player?" the great Fairbanks said, a voice now appended to the silent movie mouth, a voice hale and strong and utterly matched to the rest. But the question was caught in the wording. Did he mean a player of this game, or a player on the stage? How would he have known? In his uncertainty, Arch said nothing at all, staring.

Fairbanks burst out laughing. "Let's have a game, then," he said. Pickford, behind Fairbanks, sighed. She was small but still the undisputed star. And what contrasts! She of the milky-pale skin, under her wide-brimmed hat, as delicate as the bone china at the Grand Spa Hotel; Fairbanks, ruddy and deeply tanned, the white smile set like jewels, but oddly reminiscent of the weathered fishermen he recalled at the edges of Bristol Channel. Fairbanks was real, but regally so, or at least making the humble fisherman's tan seem kingly.

"Let's have a go, then," Fairbanks said, extending his hand. Arch took it and shook vigorously.

"I meant to hand me the cue," Fairbanks said.

The young acrobat was now firmly aground on his own mortification, unable still to summon himself. He wanted to express his adulation of this great man, but no sounds issued. Finally, he nodded and handed Fairbanks his cue.

"A silent lad, it seems," Fairbanks said. "We have, for weeks, gotten nothing but noise. The fans, screaming at all moments of the night and day."

"Relentless, really," Pickford said.

"Terrifying, actually," Fairbanks said. He laid a yellow disk on the deck and set the arc of the cue's head against it. With a small grunt he set the disk sliding. It passed the scoring triangle and came to rest a few feet past.

Arch understood enough now to get by. He laid down his own disk in an exact mimic, set his cue and duplicated Fairbanks's motion. The disk slid onto a zone numbered 7.

"Well done," Fairbanks said. "But now let's see." He set his next disk, this time looking more intent. A grunt, and the disk slid more swiftly than the first, and struck Arch's disk hard enough to knock it from its number.

"You have a name?" Fairbanks said.

"Archie."

"He does speak! And where might we be heading?"

"New York."

"Well, yes, that's where the ship seems to be going, now that I think of it," Fairbanks said. "But what's your *destination*? Is it home?" Arch was caught in a thought: That destination was a close cousin of destiny, which in this moment seemed close at hand.

"Home is behind me, sir."

"And what's in New York?"

"I'm in a troupe."

The two great actors' faces made a simultaneous *Ahhh*.

"Theater, then?"

"So to speak, sir. We're a pantomime act."

Fairbanks had clearly already lost interest in the game.

"Hold on, now! We have pantomimists in first class?"

"I might have overextended my walk a bit."

"Bully for you, boy. But how did an American come to join a British troupe?

"I'm British, sir."

"Then why do you sound American? Or more accurately, why don't you sound British?"

"I'm from the West Country, sir. It's different from London." But Arch was realizing he was already mimicking Fairbanks.

"I see. And how old are you, boy?"

"Sixteen, sir."

"Tall for sixteen. I would have taken you to be older. So you missed the war."

"I did."

"Yes, me too old, and you too young. Damned lucky, both of us."

"Indeed, sir."

"Whose place did you take?"

"Sorry, sir?"

"Someone had to go for you to arrive at such a precocious age. We always take someone else's place in this business, don't we? We're the understudies until we're not. Do you know who it was?"

"I'm not sure."

"Good. That makes it easier. I started out the same as you. I was fifteen when I joined a troupe, when another boy was called home because of his ill mother. This was in 1899. We toured the Midwest and I learned everything that was ever important. I learned how to speak well, and then I got in the pictures and learned how not to speak at all."

Arch, so accustomed in his time in the Pender Troupe to being encouraged, mentored, and handed the next opportunity, waited now for the inevitable to come.

And Fairbanks said, "So here's what I'm thinking . . ."

"Thinking can be a horribly bad habit," Pickford intoned, and not unsharply. "Doug, the boy needs to do what he needs to do."

"Very true, my dear." She was clearly ready to move on.

"Don't get yourself caught up here, young friend," Fairbanks said to Arch. "They might throw you right off the ship. I've heard on good authority that's how they treat pantomimists sneaking into first class."

"Yes, sir."

The game seemed over. They stood holding their cues upright, as if shepherds with their crooks. At the edges, people were watching, but not close enough to hear. A ship's photographer, his box camera on the end of a folded maple tripod laid across his shoulder like a long rifle, approached.

"May I, Mr. Fairbanks?" the photographer said.

"Most certainly."

"Miss Pickford as well?"

Pickford stepped to Fairbanks's side and the photographer set up his camera, then peered into the rangefinder. Then a little click. Arch heard both actors exhale.

The photographer now turned his attention to Arch, as if deciding if this young man was worthy of a photographic plate.

"Are you somebody, too?"

Arch shrugged. "Nobody at all," he said.

"This is my young British friend," Fairbanks said, grasping Arch's arm but seeming to have already forgotten his name. But Fairbanks threw his arm over Arch's shoulder, the photographer loaded a new plate and took aim, and the leaf shutter winked at him in its dark glass.

"Thank you, gentlemen," the photographer said. "And ma'am." He didn't bother to ask Arch's name, and then he was gone. That picture would be an immeasurable treasure, but he was sure he'd never see it.

Pickford looked past impatient now, wanting to move onward. Fairbanks could see that.

"Good luck, young fellow," he said, and shook Arch's hand, vigorously enough that Arch could feel his shoulder pulling at its socket. Then the great actor looked at him more intently.

"One important piece of advice, if you're going to be one of us," Fairbanks said.

"Yes, sir."

Fairbanks leaned very close and Arch suddenly got the whiff of alcohol the sea wind had taken away from a distance.

"Never touch your face. It's very bad for the skin."

Pickford gave Arch a practiced and queenly nod. And they were off, on the endless procession their fame had brought them.

Of course, Archie knew exactly whom he'd replaced. This had been early in his stint with Pender, and with the Great War still smoldering on. Arch wanted to believe his indisputable talent was what prompted Pender to bring on such a young trainee. Even with "the hostilities" having dragged on for so long, boys still moved on, one body replacing another at the front, and another replacing that body on the stage. As a Boy Scout (Bristol Falcons; Bob Bennett, troop leader) aged twelve, Arch had been conscripted as a volunteer messenger at Southampton. There, the troop ships loaded up with legions of boys whose smiling bravado faltered slightly, but visibly, as they trod that rattling gangplank, to steam toward France and the death fields and the stalemated, rat-filled trenches. And he saw those ships simultaneously offloading boys the other way, many of them missing arms and legs, some with skin scarred by fire, and even those physically unscathed with their eyes indelibly marked by the experience. He thought those intersecting lines reminded him of the dual masks of the theater, not exactly Comedy and Tragedy, but rather anticipation and tragic deliverance.

When he'd arrived with the Pender Troupe, at fourteen years of age, he looked at the sixteen-year-olds as being impossibly more sophisticated in their practice of the physical arts. Lean, agile, fearless, confident. On stilts, on ropes, in tumbles and falls that never seemed to hurt them, forming their human pyramids as solid as cut stone. They were young masters of a skill that daunted Arch even in his eagerness to acquire it. He waited his turn, and like everything in those war years, the turn came quickly enough. Two of them, Handy and Reed, were among those to go, shortly after Arch's arrival. But the true younger star of the troupe was Charnley, a seventeen-year-old Arch could instantly see had a bearing beyond all others, and a charisma that glowed hot in the lights, but who also had a quiet but clear aversion to having anything to do with this war, or any other.

Charnley rarely spoke. He fascinated Arch in the tamped-down heat of his devotion to the comic virtuosity. He never seemed to smile. He was a sharply handsome boy, nearly dour, not some rubberface who mugged to get a laugh. The girls in the troupe were well aware of his attractiveness. But taught to be ladylike, they dared not approach him. All expression came from his tight movements. Charnley tumbled majestically, the air of danger and inevitable injury fully expressed, then abruptly defied. Arch always watched him intently, and when it came to Arch's own turn, he tried to visualize himself as if at a distance—out of body, yet matching the immediate sensation of being inside the tumble, watching the floor spin around him, its surface rolling down his back like a wheel and then him finding his feet. There was an acquired logic to the motion that had to fight the inner ears' shrill alarms. Then Pender's barking instructions and adjustments—*No, no, your shoulders like this . . . we don't need any broken necks 'round here*—until the perfection of each linking action locked in and made the movement whole.

Arch never tried to ingratiate himself to Charnley, and Charnley made little effort to befriend Arch or anyone else. He was at an altogether different level. Even the older boys seemed to stand in awe of Charnley, in a way that seemed to make him both untouchable and unapproachable. Pender, even, gave him his respectful due.

Then Charnley arrived on a particular morning looking drained of his blood. As quiet as he had always been, he was now somehow quieter; he was nearly shivering. One sort of courage did not so easily convert to another, it seemed; this was not an exchange of pounds for francs. Danger had many faces and many rewards.

The conscription papers had come. Charnley was about to turn eighteen, but maybe he thought he'd somehow go unnoticed. Or perhaps he'd hoped the war would end suddenly, and specifically, to spare him.

Pender acted as if he didn't notice any of it. He put the boys straight to work. Action purged rumination. Attention riveted to the tight sequences of movement left no room for anything else. But Charnley had gone instantly bad. He suddenly couldn't do anything, and this proved frightening to Arch. Pender himself seemed briefly aghast, then went blank. Arch later realized Pender, in this juncture, had given up on Charnley, just like that. Charnley was a short-timer who couldn't recover his mastery. His tumbles lost their tightness, a watchspring sprung; his landings were hesitant, shaky, no longer planted so firmly. Bob Pender would normally have had much to say about such miscues, but instead he just watched.

On an otherwise unremarkable morning, Charnley was gone. Pender said nothing about it. He simply eyed his younger charges, then stuck a thick finger at Arch and said, "You, then." And so it was. He was their new Charnley-in-waiting now.

Arch accepted it. He embraced it, really, with nary a whit of concern about the real Charnley's fate. He really never gave him another thought, too intent on grasping the moment. Arch's own tumbling and stilt-walking suddenly felt right, deft, mysteriously informed. Pender watched and went silent again, but now because he was devoid of criticisms. Equilibrium had been restored. Arch found himself retreating to those quieter spaces once held by Charnley. He was trying on a personality, like a fresh-pressed suit. The other boys took a quiet step back. The troupe was divided into a better and lesser unit. He'd already been the better of the lesser; now he was promoted to a lesser of the better. In time, Pender switched things up, and Arch had made his way to being one of the best of the better.

The act was always changing things up. They worked up a bit in stilts, dressed up like puppets with bulbous heads; the stilts on each acrobat were longer than the next, and where Arch had started off on the three-footers, by the end he was on the twelve-footers, the tallest of the array, and terrifying. On those, he was the showstopper when he entered the stage to the audience's predictable delight. Spying through the narrow eyeholes of his puppet's head, he danced by feel, the troupe's movements so precisely choreographed that they never collided. That was the key—the practicing of tight quarters and a passion for utter exactness—be it a dance, a tumbling sequence, or an aerial.

That summer, the troupe went up to Colwyn Bay on the Welsh coast, performing on the long pier. They went to Folkstone and Hastings and Weymouth and Margate, the summer towns, playing wherever there was a stage or a hall or a bit of open land on which to gather an audience. And then as the autumn set in, on to all the bigger towns and stages of the region.

Armistice came that November. The troupe was solidified; Arch and Bob Pender's younger brother, Tommy, became friends. Over the holidays and into the early winter, when the troupe was not on tour, Arch and the younger boys stayed on at the Penders' home in Brixton. He began to feel a little more like he had found a family.

The summer of 1919, the rumors abruptly circulated that Charnley had died in battle. Two out of every three retellings suggested it was really quite heroic. The story had arisen without proof, documentation, or purpose. No one could provide any details or even arrive at the source of this disclosure: It was just something that had been going around. The war had been over for nearly a year; indeed, Charnley had never been seen again. His absence seemed proof enough. People simply didn't not come home, if they could. Whether it was true or not, the fact remained that without Charnley's effective erasure, Arch knew he would not have gotten his chance so early on. Had the war ended just months earlier, Charnley would still be the headliner in the troupe, and perhaps on to bigger things. Pender never spoke of these rumors, and no one ever had the courage to ask.

And so on a July morning in 1920, standing on the deck of the *Olympic*, his unplayed shuffleboard disk at his feet, he watched Fairbanks recede, tipping his boater at passersby, receiving their adulation. Pickford seemed braced for the moment, maybe not quite as comfortable when negotiating the world at its true size. It was as if something was radiating from them, as though in rear projection. Now, Arch had been seen by, and touched by, and acknowledged by another man he was now intending to replace.

As the *Olympic* slid slowly toward its berth at the White Star pier, Pender had his troupe queued underdecks with their suitcases and duffels, frank in his own excitement. They stood on the white-painted iron expanse of a portside E Deck alleyway as the ship's laborers stood at the open portal, hand-signaling to the workers arrayed below on Pier 59. The women of the troupe had been sent to another gangway with Mrs. Pender, and Mr. Pender had instructed them all to meet at the pier's hemispheric main entrance.

"We'll be going right to the theater, all, right to work," he said.

"When you get outside, don't step in the traffic—there's good reason they call it Death Avenue, I'm told."

But they could barely hear him. They'd stood at the rail until the last possible moment marveling at New York City on this humid morning, listening to the distant screech of the streetcars on their rails and the automobile horns volleying back and the sound of wind blowing through the buildings. The sun, orange in the morning haze, shone between the high buildings.

"Don't be gawky, now," Pender shouted now. "Look smart and keep your heads up. We're hardly here on bloody holiday!"

One of the other boys, Billy, murmured behind Arch that "we'll bloody well see about that."

Pender turned.

"Archie, what say you?"

"I said we'll bloody well see to that, sir!"

Pender nodded at him and then turned to the others, "See, boys, one of us is here to make his mark. I hope all of you take on that attitude!"

"What a josser," Billy said more softly, and Arch wasn't quite sure of whom he was speaking. "Once I'm on land, I'm not going back."

"How so?" Arch said.

"This is the place. Everything's happening here."

"Don't you need some sort of . . . permission?"

"From who? Bob? He'll be right with it."

"What about papers?"

"All we need is our actors' visas. They don't expire for three years."

"I didn't know you could stay with those . . ."

"So now you know."

The ropes were thrown and the tugs churned below, with their bullish ministrations. The dockworkers on the pier were close enough that Arch could see their sour faces as they waited, some resting with their arms folded and propped over the gangway rails, which were sided with bleached canvas on which were painted in black *Cunard White Star*. It was just another day of hard labor that belied the singular momentousness Arch felt.

The ship finally stopped, and the engines ceased for the first time since England. The gangway lines came up and the Pender troupe watched the ship's laborers put their shoulders into the work, lifting the ramp with groans and curses. They sounded Irish, Arch thought, condemned to the endless physical drudgery. He could hear the crowd on the pier now, shouting to the ship, maybe seeing the loved one they were here to receive, or just emoting at the great ship's presence. People waiting for people, happy at their safe passage. The *Titanic* was eight years gone, but its horrors lived in memory and kept people on edge right until a ship made shore.

The gangway hooks were slowly set, and one of the Irishmen kicked at it to test its solidity. Everyone pressed in a bit closer now, waiting for the all-clear. America now lay just at the bottom of the ramp. Arch felt the churn, and as well he fought the momentary pang of having no one at all, ahead or behind, no commitments or responsibilities, no firm ground or forbidden territories. And for a long time now. And he could remember the precise moment this feeling began, the day when his life had begun to both empty and fill.

ecognition

TODAY HE TAKES AN *unexpected journey. He is walking in a city, which city he is not so sure, or when, or why.*

He's passing through crowds, the lively bustle of the throngs. He's always favored cities, and their energy; rarely, though, is he out walking by himself. But here he finds himself.

And he's slowly realizing he sees no other men. In this instant, he's amused at the anomaly, of passing through a randomly sorted cluster of women, and sets his mind for waiting for the men to begin to appear in the crowd. But they don't, for quite some time.

No, it's ladies, young and old, all manner of height and weight and color and expression. Some are seemingly serene in their thoughts, faces with just-curling smiles at some rumination. Others seem to carry the troubled expressions of pressure and weight. Here and there, a couple of women might be in conversation, but as in most cities, the greater whole walk alone. But he feels oddly at home.

No one at all seems to notice him. These women glide by, busy in their lives, lost in their cohort. And none seems to even notice him.

He doesn't seem to stand out at all. He holds no apparent attraction. He pivots toward a plate-glass storefront window and sees his dark reflection, and that he is as he should be. A tall and handsome man in an impeccable suit. Yet he moves along as if a wraith, transparent and noiseless.

So he continues on, growing aware now that he has no apparent destination. But he's also aware that he's looking for a familiar face in this sea of women. Seeking anyone he knows, and yet seeking someone very specific. He sees women who remind him of someone familiar but are not. One woman passing in the opposite direction looks like his own mother, but as a young woman. As he gets closer he sees that it is not. She has not so much as a flicker of recognition as she brushes past him.

But ahead, another woman, much older and just as familiar, but as she gets closer, the recognition again fades. He doesn't exactly know who he's looking for, or how to know her, yet he is determined for that to happen.

The crowd on the street is dense, shoulder to shoulder and feet moving and flowing in both directions, entangling and navigating.

And so he must keep on, with no chance to stop. He is unclear as to where the flow will take him. It occurs to him he's not even sure he's going the right way.

1959

IN THE DAY'S SESSION of the Treatment, in colors that even Hitchcock could never produce on a silver screen, he envisions his penis as a rocket ship, roaring into space. He feels the heat and light and noise, a powerful thing; it is neither elating or disturbing, just what seems a fact. As real as his hand in front him. In the follow-up, he tells Dr. Hartman about it.

"Should I worry about that?"

"That's not as unusual as you might surmise," the doctor says.

"Other men see their penises as rockets?"

"Not exactly, but people will see many things. As you know by now."

"Of course, these spaceships have an astronaut, don't they?"

"Was there an astronaut?"

"There was, and it was me. I was the pilot of the rocket that was my penis. And most certainly, I myself have a penis. So it becomes a Russian-doll sort of affair, as it were."

"The image seems to be important to you."

"Is it male pride, I wonder? I suppose a rocket has a destination, or a rendezvous."

"Or is it a mission?"

"Of destruction?"

"Interesting you think that. Perhaps exploration. Perhaps for a greater good."

"'To serve man,' and whatnot."

"Your rocket has served your own needs, but what are the new realities?"

"Now, Doctor, are we still discussing my penis?"

"We're discussing your visions. Your thoughts. The mind constructs scenarios to help you see the truth you might not want to admit."

"But I have no idea what it means!"

"Perhaps it will be revealed in time."

"It will be exposed, if you will . . ."

The doctor smiles. "Cleverness is a fine shield, isn't it? No one even realizes you're defending."

"That's the trick, isn't it?"

"So as we examine this vision, we must also recognize that even a high-flying object must yet come down to earth. So the shield must be there, to withstand the heat and friction."

"We really are extending this phallic metaphor, aren't we?"

"There's the humor again. The perfect self-protection."

The Acrobat is quiet for a moment, then speaks.

"These feel like dreams," he says. "How are they different?"

"The difference is that the things you see during treatment, and the places you go, are places you choose to see and to go, even if you don't want to . . ."

At night, he finds, when he's in his pajamas and settled in, the rocket is rarely in a mode to launch anymore. As at Cape Canaveral, conditions seem more favorable in the mornings. A concession to his aging, he expects; he'd been with Betsy so long—by far his longest marriage—he's presumed that easy comfort was part of it as well. But the comfort has become the discomfort. As always. He's lived through every marriage in fear of her vanishing. And so he always left first, even if in spirit. He forced things as he wished them to happen.

He'd spent two weeks eager for another session. And sometimes when he's finally there, on the couch, with the magic coursing through his synapses, nothing much happens. He wonders if such placid visions signal some movement toward more-placid existence, or whether the particular dose is simply a dud, like an unexploded firecracker.

But Dr. Hartman, whom he has dubbed "the Swami," has assured him before that Sandoz Labs does not produce duds, and does not produce inconsistencies, not like the street-sold, homemade versions that are giving the Treatment a bad name as they spread among the beatniks and the jazz scene. Even the Sandoz tablets, as meticulously produced as fine Swiss watches, spark wildly different reactions. The Swami attributes this not to the drug but to the state of mind it has entered. But the doctor sometimes offers a quote.

"As is said, 'Someday this pain may be useful to you,'" he'd offered at the beginning of today's journey.

"Who said that?"

"Ovid."

"As is also said, 'It is always by pain that one arrives at pleasure.'"

"Is that Ovid as well?"

"No, it's the Marquis de Sade."

But no pain arrived, and Dr. Hartman told him afterward that the Treatment was only half the equation.

"The treatment meets your subconscious on equal terms," he said, "and your mind is not so much acted upon but rather made a partner in a dance. It will reveal your missteps and also bring out the finer flourishes one didn't even know one had."

"The music didn't even play today," the Acrobat said.

"And sometimes it may be the case that we're working up to something rather monumental."

He has the television in his bedroom and when he dares to turn it on, it issues like a firehose, from dawn to the wee hours. *Gunsmoke. Bonanza. The Texan.* What's the sudden allure of all these television cowboys? Even Hitch has succumbed and fronted a television show. It nearly seems self-sabotage for a movie director, but the man seems to love the camera time, for someone who claims not to be an actor.

The Acrobat recalls the sweet agony of his childhood, when he had to wait patiently for the new pictures to show up at the Metropole out on Ashley Road. The Metropole was a one-tier hall, made simple for the simple joy of the moving picture. A new show was hardly an everyday occurrence in far-flung Bristol, which meant long intervals of boredom. Radio had not yet arrived; his home was not a place where books might have reasonably been found. His taciturn mother told no stories; his hungover father saved his tales for his pub mates. For a child, going to the movies was a place to discover the human race.

Now, via a box in his bedroom, he is drowning in it.

He tends to avoid watching news as much as he once did; so much has become so dismaying. The government just fired a monkey into the sky, poor doomed Gordo, to match the dogs the Russians keep rocketing upward; apparently there's a succession of primates set to go, Able and Baker and so on. And seven men will shortly be chosen to replace the monkeys. He has rockets on his mind constantly, for some reason. And the pictures seemed swallowed up by science fiction, as cars look more like spaceships and houses are beginning to look like the lunar bases from those terrible D-movies. Frank Lloyd Wright is landing a Martian spacecraft on the Upper East Side of New York in the form of the Guggenheim Museum.

"I'm not saying any of this is a bad thing," he had said in a recent phone call to Howard Hughes as the TV flashed on without volume. "I'm just saying I'm a bit slow to adjust."

"As I am," Howard said from his bungalow at the Beverly Hills Hotel, from which he had not emerged in nearly a year. "It's a world I'm not sure I know anymore."

"I should come by and see you. I'm here at Beverly Drive right now. I'm five minutes away if you need me. I'm leaving for Florida in a few days to start a new picture, but we should have lunch."

"No, let's not. I really can't see anybody these days. Much too busy."

"Well, I thought I'd try."

"Off to make another picture, then."

"Always another picture, Howard. Just a light comedy. It fits me like an old shoe. And it will certainly make money."

"I don't follow the business much. After I got rid of RKO, I'd had enough of it—the commies, that bastard Walt Disney, all of it. They were all against me. I had to pull back, you know."

The Acrobat has indeed heard, from friends, about how Howard in 1958 had isolated himself in a screening room and wouldn't come out for four months. Howard, his former best man. His partner in crime, sexual and otherwise, once upon a very long time ago.

"We had such fun in the old days, though, Howard."

"The old days are the old days, my friend. I prefer to avoid it all."

"Well, I plan the opposite. I want to meet things head-on."

"To each his own, I'd say."

"People change, Howard. The world changes. I'm trying to embrace that. My treatment is helping me."

"Why you would ingest these chemicals is beyond me. Nothing is clean anymore. Don't you understand that? Food isn't safe. They irradiate milk now, you know."

"I hear it makes it safer."

"That's want they want you to hear."

"To each his own. So you won't drink milk. Hitch is terrified of eggs, you know. And I myself am quite concerned about cocktail onions. I simply refuse to eat them."

"You think this is all amusing?"

"I'm just trying hard to be an optimist, old friend. Are you quite all right, Howard?"

"The fact is, I'm getting ruined by jet engines."

"Pardon?"

"I've put all of TWA's money into turboprops, which are

clearly superior devices. But everyone wants jet engines now."

"Well, they do go faster, I hear."

"And they cost more. And they waste fuel. Doesn't anyone want to go a little slower and save a lot of money on their ticket?"

"We live in increasingly fast times, I'd say."

Silence on the end of the line.

"I'm going to lose this company, and you're telling me the obvious," Howard said.

"Howard, what's happened to you? Are you really quite all right? You stood up for me, and I feel as if I should be concerned."

"I was more than your best man, and I can't see what you're concerned about. Why aren't you concerned about yourself?"

"How do you mean?"

"However you think I mean. That's for you to figure out. I have enough problems of my own."

1917

THE ACTS THAT CAME through the Empire were by definition second-rate, but a fair number of them had once upon on a time been first-rate. Fading stars attracted crowds more than rising stars, and marquees depended on recognizable names. And so to Arch's surprise, the Great Devant came to Bristol. Further surprising was that Arch was told he'd be working the arc light for Devant's act.

Devant was an illusionist of the highest order, or at least had once been. He'd given command performances for both Edward VII and George V, and had tread the boards of the London Palace and Egyptian Hall. Why such a famous performer was coming to the Empire, and not down by the river at the Hippodrome, indicated some special place in his heart for the little barn—at least according to Melvyn, the aged gent who tended the stage door.

"I knew him back in the old days, but he won't remember me," Melvyn had said as he manned the door, awaiting Devant's arrival. "He's a fine fellow, let me tell you." He told Arch that the magician would confer with him to discuss the lighting, and that this was a golden chance to meet a true great.

Somewhere around the dinner hour, a taxi pulled up at the stage door. A tall and mustached man lugging a heavy suitcase stepped out, gingerly, onto the rain-washed cobbles. He came to the doorway, where Melvyn was waiting, clearly nervous. Devant smiled broadly and then shook Melvyn's hand vigorously. "Hallo, friend!" he said. Arch wasn't sure Devant actually recognized Melvyn, but Melvyn was clearly convinced he had.

The best dressing room was for the headliner, to which Devant followed Melvyn. "I have two assistants coming in on the next train," he said. "They're bringing more of the same."

"Have you done the Empire before?" Melvyn asked.

"I've never had to," Devant said. "A sign of my slow decline, I'm afraid."

"It's not so bad a place," Melvyn said.

"I'm quite happy to gather any audience that will still have me," Devant said, as he eased his suitcase down onto the floor. "My literal bag of tricks. Please don't anyone touch it. Treat it as if it's a basket full of eggs."

Melvyn said, "I remember you from St. George's Hall. We did a bit just before you. I did Hamlet's soliloquy while me partner mimed it up. Do we remember that?"

Devant looked briefly shocked, and then his grin went wide. He was remembering someone now, and fondly.

"I adored that act, for its complete madness! You brought the house down with that!" He stood and went to Melvyn and abruptly hugged him. "Old friend, truly! The old times!"

"Have us a drink," Melvyn said, "for reminiscence."

Devant turned to Arch and said, "This man was truly wonderful." He turned back to Melvyn. "Are you still performing?"

"No more of that," Melvyn said. "Here, I serve as something of a *majordome*, a kind of *gardien de la maison*."

"Well done, then," the magician said. Melvyn then produced a not-insubstantial bottle from his clothing, not an unmagical feat.

"Only two drinks before a show, and never within the hour," Devant said. Then he looked at Arch.

"Come back at seven with the others, and we'll make the plan," he said. "The talk for now will be of old and happy times, and that will seem tedious to you, as it is to all who are fortunate enough to be young. And how did you end up at the Empire at such a tender age?"

The answer would have been too long to attempt, and he sensed the question was rhetorical. It had begun three years before, with the disappearance of his mother.

That memory was as burned in as a scar: through the door that day, home from school, another rain-soaked day. His father sitting in his usual chair at a very unusual time of day. Elias was a tailor's presser at the Todd's factory, who at best came home from work for dinner, and very often didn't. He loved the pub and mostly left Arch, nine years old, to his brooding, silent mother.

Father was, as always, dressed well; his philosophy was that one was better to wear a threadbare suit that was once exquisite than to wear a new suit that wasn't well-made. Elias Leach had an odd look on his face, neither sad nor angry, but somehow weighted. Arch could not hear a sound in the house beyond the creak of the chair on which his father shifted.

"Where's Mum?" Arch said hesitantly. As it turned out, this was the subject at hand.

"Your mother," he said. "She's had to go away."

"Where?"

"To the seaside."

"Are we going to the seaside, too?"

"No."

"For how long?"

His father seemed not to have expected questions. "For a while."

"When will she come back?"

"Not for some time. That's that, then. I need to be back at work," his father said. Elias stared at Arch, as if waiting for the boy to speak. Which he did not. "You can find some food around here, can't you?"

Arch nodded. His father stood.

"Very well then, I'm off," Elias said, making for the door as if in retreat.

That was it. And the absence was not just his mother's. His home was a house full of absences: his father's in body, his mother's in spirit, and one other in any existence at all. He had, in small increments, become vaguely aware of a child who had passed away. John. Dead before Arch was born. Never mentioned, but always present in all their days. Can that even be your brother if you never walked in the same world? John was never spoken of; Arch had learned in small clues and realizations. The baby in the picture that lay facedown in his mother's drawer. The documents kept locked in a box. The tamped-down grief that couldn't find a voice.

He saw very little of his father from then on. Arch rose in the morning for school as his father slept, and fell asleep long before his father came stumbling home. His grandmother, his father's mother, appeared from time to time at first. She was a birdlike woman who clucked and worried and in time mostly exited.

Money was doled him in small allotments on the table. Arch foraged and did without to make more use of those small coins, precious to him: More and more, Arch fled the silence of his home for the noise of the movie house, where he could be insulated in the laughter as Chaplin, Keaton, and Linder lit up the screen in their silent glories.

By the time he was thirteen, he came and went as he pleased. His mother had now been on her holiday at the seaside for nearly four years. She had by now been consigned and mostly forgotten, like pictures laid facedown in a dusty drawer.

School held no interest for him. He had friends but that didn't seem enough: He'd joined the Boy Scouts. He ran with his schoolyard chums. He flirted with girls, who at times boldly flirted back. And he found his way to the shows.

At the Bristol Hippodrome, the live shows had a charged roughness to them, and he could be among people instead of an abandoned home. Strangers all around him, looking for a diversion from war and privation. People of all ages except for the pointed absence of young men, all off to fight. Gaggles of teenaged girls came together, and in the lobby he could overhear them speaking of boys they knew, and the letters that came from France and Belgium, where the fronts were stalemated and the conflict had no end in sight. But being in an audience felt too passive a fate for him. He insinuated himself backstage, but was turned away by an electrician, who said—with an unmistakable tone of dismissiveness—to try the Empire.

He walked right down. The main entrance of the Empire Palace of Varieties faced Old Market, but the red stage door was around the corner on Captain Carey's Lane. The door was loosely secured, as the performers were not much sought after and hardly celebrities. The only regulation was to keep people from bypassing the ticket booth, so the vigilance dissipated once the show was well under way. This old fellow Melvyn watching the door, when he wasn't wandering. Melvyn was a man with a bulbous and pocked nose and wispy hair that might have once been red. On a particular night when Melvyn had drifted, Arch stepped through the portal and waited patiently to be seen.

When Melvyn eventually came limping back around, he howled as if Arch were setting the place on fire.

"What the faffing hell do you think you're doing, boy?"

"I'm looking for work."

"Here? Well, I don't know about that."

"Why not? I need the money."

"You look awfully green. How old are you?"

"What does that matter? I can do anything you need. I've been a Boy Scout, you know."

"Well, aren't we the nuts, then? A fully capable Nancy in his starchy suit."

"I can't help it. My father's a presser."

"And where is he as we speak?"

"Out on a piss, just like every night. Down the pub."

"A presser and a drunkard. Hope not at the same time. So the boy has good looks and no money, then."

"That sums it up nicely."

Melvyn laughed then.

"Where do you live?"

"Horfield."

"That's a jaunt."

"For you, maybe."

Melvyn laughed again.

"Well don't you go to school?"

"The Fairfield Grammar School."

"Not bad for a presser's boy."

"I couldn't say. They gave me a scholarship I didn't want. Mostly out of pity."

"And your mum?"

"Long gone. She went away and never came back. That's why the pity."

Melvyn nodded.

"Well, then. No jobs to be had right now. But maybe come back tomorrow."

So Arch returned the next night. Once again, old Melvyn was on the prowl, so Arch waited just inside the door. The backstage area was thrifty, like the stage itself, with counterweights and banks of lights and the milling clutches of performers waiting in the shadows to go on. Fairfield Grammar could hold no candle to this.

When Melvyn spotted him, he motioned him to wait. He returned with an officious-looking woman whom he introduced as Mrs. Stevens. She looked Arch up and down, and said, "You can work for no pay."

"All right."

"If you do well enough, then the money."

"All right."

So instead of being thrown out, he was put straight to work. Mrs. Stevens was not seen again, perhaps confined to the business office, but Melvyn introduced him to everyone else. Melvyn had been a trouper, in the music hall days of the 1870s and on.

"I played Canterbury, Wilton's, and the Old Mo on Drury Lane," Melvyn would tell all who would listen, most of whom had no clue what those references meant. "A fellow would need to be a mime at one turn, and recite Shakespeare the next."

The limp, he said, "was simply a matter of overusing myself.

Watch out for that. Don't burn the wick too quick!"

And so Arch avoided burning the wick by more carefully rationing his time in school. Feigned illnesses and forged notes. Teachers seemed alarmed at first, then seemed to stop caring. He'd become a lost cause. That was fine by him. He'd never been much for school and its silent passivity. Besides, he had so much to learn.

On the hour, Arch knocked softly on the dressing-room door. He heard only a murmur of assent, and he eased the door open. Melvyn had returned to his post at the stage door, and the Great Devant was in his chair, hunched over and kneading his right hand with his left. There was now a much larger case next to his suitcase, and a young man, not quite as young as Arch, sat silently on a stool.

"This is Malcolm," Devant said. "My other assistant is Alice, who has gone to prepare herself."

Malcolm nodded to Arch and murmured, "Hallo."

Devant seemed lost in thought, but then he said without looking up, "How old are you?"

"Sixteen, sir."

"I'll take you on your word. How long have you run an arc light?"

"A year, sir."

"A year, in the same way that you're sixteen?"

Arch said nothing. Devant tightened his hands into fists, then opened them.

"My bloody hands confound me," the magician said.

Arch had no idea.

"They go numb," he said. "They shake. Ever since the war began. Though that may just be coincidence. I wasn't actually in the war, of course."

He was opening and closing his fingers, making the fists and then popping them open like starfish.

"My understanding is that you'll run the follow spot, yes?"

"Yes, sir."

"Here's what I will want you to do," Devant said. "Don't hold the light too tightly on my hands. Because of this shaking. Yes, that is the place where the trick happens, but I'll have you widen out a bit so it might take away a bit of the attention. Say, from here to here," he said, and with that he spread his arms nearly fully.

"Yes, sir."

"Be very aware that my props will be concealed behind me. There are some small mirrors you must avoid. Be very precise. Keep the light above my waist."

"Yes, sir."

"All right, then." Devant looked at his hands again. "It's just the damnedest thing," he said, mostly to himself.

After leaving the dressing room so Devant could prepare, Malcolm quietly sat with Arch and the main light technician, a gray man named Walter. Malcolm went through the list of tricks and the lighting for each. Walter had the real job, with several lights at his command; Arch had the follow, which was to frame the magician. A simple job.

Arch climbed the ladder as the audience found its seats below. He settled into the lighting perch to sit in the darkness waiting for the show. He felt like a sparrow tucked into the eaves, not to be noticed as the audience began to settle themselves in their places. When the band in the pit seated themselves and began to tune, Arch waited behind his rig. It was a beastly device, a two-hundred-pound cylinder of steel and iron on a swivel, hotter than a coal stove once it was lighted. It had a small tin chimney on its top to release the heat, but working the light meant to be soaked in sweat by show's end. He needed to set the carbon rods and then adjust them as they burned, lest the arc died. Looking into the carbon vapor was nearly blinding, but Walter, across the balcony operating the wider lights, had taught him the elements and intoned more than once, "Never touch the metal, or you'll carry it the rest of your life."

With the stage still dark and awaiting the first cue, Arch had the now-familiar interlude of coldness, and had come to understand its pleasure in the waning moments before curtain. He touched the cylinder and it was like a block of ice. But as the band struck up and the curtains began to open with the first act, a comedic singer stage-named Sophie Sweet, Arch snapped the lever to ignite the arc. The heat and light was instant, the punishing flames of Hades screaming through every seam. Steam rose from the light's chimney and he got the brief smell of burning dust. Arch took the insulated handles of the light and trained the beam downward, through the haze of the cigarette smoke rising from the audience, onto the performer upon whom all eyes were fixed.

Arch ran the lights by rote for most of the acts, house performers he'd seen many times. Devant was scheduled toward the end, and Arch felt a bit of rising excitement, for an act that had gone before the royals. Through the clatter of the usual fare, he waited.

And then, the introduction, and the tightened grip on the handles, and the curtain rising to Devant amid his apparatus. Devant, top-hatted and tuxedoed and smiling broadly, a different man than he'd seen in the dressing room.

"What a sublime pleasure to be back at the Empire once again," he said. "I've performed in the great halls and before the crowned heads, but being back here feels, always, like a return to a warm home."

The audience applauded and Arch took note.

The first trick was something Devant called his "Gollywog Ball." He set up a small wooden ramp, took out a small white ball, and let the ball roll down the ramp, finishing with a flourish that indicated that was the extent of the trick. The audience sat silently.

"Well, aren't you a demanding lot," he said. "The nobility was always quite pleased with that trick. They couldn't bloody figure it out, really . . ." Now the roar came, and Devant walked to the low end of the ramp, placed the ball there, and let go. Now the ball rolled up the ramp through no visible means. The audience now applauded, and Devant smiled and bowed. "For a moment there, I'd worried about the gravity of this proceeding," he said, to a bigger laugh.

And on to more tricks. Alice appeared, a thin girl with a face paled by powder, assisting with the illusions. Devant was businesslike, moving from trick to trick in a way that spoke of a man who had done them thousands of times before. The man, on stage, was airy and seeming to be without a worry in the world. Malcolm stayed mostly behind the back curtain, preparing each new trick and pushing them through the divide.

"Now, I've found of late that my chickens are coming home to roost," he said. "I'm an older fellow now, and I find I need to mind my eggs." He reached into his coat and pulled out a large wicker basket, to the audience's astonishment.

"Let's see now . . ." he said. He fumbled through his pockets and brought out an egg, then another, then another. From the other pocket as many. He was filling the basket and the audience was with him. He reached down to his shoe and pulled out two more, seemingly out of the sole. The trick was about quantity; the basket was filling, and as Devant pulled a couple more from his armpit, one slipped from his grip. It exploded across the stage, and the audience cried out.

Devant smiled. "Just part of the act," he said.

And finally, Malcolm rolled out the large suitcase he had arrived with. He had a dark cape on his arm, and he helped Devant put it over his shoulders.

"Time for Alice to get home," Devant said, opening the case. Alice stepped in and lithely folded herself down into it. Malcolm had explained the trick, and how Alice would suddenly turn up from the wings.

Arch was leaning forward to see if he could figure out how the trick worked. Devant shut the lid on Alice and snapped the locks, and Arch was watching for movement. He was almost sure what was going to happen when there was a louder gasp from the crowd. He looked back at Devant and saw that a glaring beam of light was reflecting onto the crowd, and he couldn't tell where it was coming from. But as he moved his own light, that light moved as well. He realized what he'd just done.

"He's got a bloody mirror behind him!" a man in the crowd shouted, seemingly not for spite but more just feeling clever to have figured it out. Alice was wrapped in dark cloth she must have got into inside the suitcase, and was trying to roll under the back curtain before she was noticed. But she was spotted as well. The laughter rose, and Devant looked up at Arch, a beseeching look, and then looked to someone in the wings and made the familiar knife-across-the-throat gesture. The front curtain dropped heavily as the crowd roared, until the last act, a trained dog and its master, trotted out to salvage the night.

In the dressing room, Devant had the bottle out and was pouring. He said, "No need to limit it now. Long train ride home."

Melvyn, as if at a wake, poured himself a dram. He'd brought in Archie, who was to sit in silence until called upon.

"My days grow short upon the stage," Devant said. "Tonight

was just distraction."

Melvyn gave Arch the nod then.

"Sir, I want to apologize for my mistake."

Devant looked at Arch with a mild smile. "How old are you, in true fact?"

"Thirteen, sir."

"You were fairly good for most of it. A mistake to learn by, I'd say."

Arch felt as if he were going to burst into tears but pulled it back.

"Well, there's the one thing," Melvyn said to Arch. "Word from upstairs is you're sacked. Sorry, boy."

"They weren't even paying me," Arch said generally.

Melvyn shrugged. "Go to the Hippodrome, and tell them about everything you've done here, except tonight."

Devant looked into his drink and said, "The wonderful thing about show business is everybody bungs it up once in a while."

Arch nodded. "Sir, was dropping the egg part of the act?"

"Of course it wasn't part of the act," Devant said. "At the end, I'm supposed to crack it into my hat and then put my hat back on, to no adverse effect. But that, alas, was my one real egg."

The Hippodrome's need for warm bodies had apparently increased since he'd last come around. Or maybe he now had the bearing of an experienced hand. The stage manager put him straight to work, for pay that was abysmal but clearly a raise from the Empire.

Arch continued to make himself handy. Carrying messages, loading wardrobe, fetching food and covering the door. In the last of these tasks, he was in the best place to acquaint himself with the many faces of the local scene. In time, he was standing at the stage door when Bob Pender and his rowdy knockabouts came bursting in from London, and he saw his future.

"Are you looking for anyone?" he asked Pender, who in his attire looked more a smiling banker than a showman.

"We're always looking for somebody good," Pender said. "But we don't always find them."

Late that night, after the show, Pender walked Arch out onto the stage and said, "Are you sixteen?"

"Certainly I am."

"Let's see what you can do, then." And then Arch did it, as impromptu an action as he'd ever taken, informed by the endless hours of watching the acts from behind the arc light. Pender watched silently, then nodded for Arch to stop.

"You're left-handed?"

"Yes, sir. Does it matter?"

"It might. But I suppose we can make some use of you. And you are sixteen, correct?"

"Almost."

Arch was not yet fourteen, not old enough to legally leave school.

"I'll just need a letter of permission from your parents," Pender said.

"Straight away," Arch said.

"And what's with your mouth?"

"Knocked a tooth out."

"Smile for me, if you will."

Arch did so.

"Keep that gob shut tight, then," Pender said. "Learn to breathe through your nose."

Writing the letter to Pender was easy: Arch was already tall, and he felt, by circumstances thrust upon him, that he was an older boy and was merely relieving his father of the task. As with the British Army during the war, who seemed to take enlistees at

55

their word, he found no reason to think Pender would challenge his facts. When he dropped the letter into the pillar box by the school, he felt but a step away from freedom. Intercepting Pender's reply in the mail became the greater challenge. He hovered daily by the front door, waiting. The day that letter arrived (accepting him and including train fare to Brixton), he packed quickly, left without emotion, and was convinced his father was never going to notice his absence. His father had a woman now. She lived not far away, and she was pregnant, a child to replace him. On the train, he realized his one oversight, that the small coins his father left for him on the table would begin to accumulate, signaling his absence. But for the rest of the ride, he convinced himself his father would shed no tears for him, as Elias had shed no tears for Mother. Arch had long since come to intuit that his mother had died. His father's new family (though Elias remained unmarried) seemed to confirm that. So who was Arch? Someone for whom going away, and being someone else, was the best course.

And for two glorious weeks, he believed he had made it work.

He and the other new boys were billeted in a small room off the kitchen of the Pender home. Four of them, whom the Penders always awakened early. It was like the military, a rigor to firmly engage their apprenticeship. But on this morning, as the four boys pulled themselves out of their cots to queue sleepily by the loo, Bob Pender said, "Archie, wait now." When the others were out of the room, he shut the door.

"I heard from your father," Pender said. "Says he never wrote that letter. He tells me you're a tad younger than you had allowed."

Pender's tone seemed devoid of any anger, almost con-spiratorial. "You almost had me, and I might have been willing to look the other way. But I don't ever stand between boys and their fathers."

"Is he taking me away?"

"He's in the parlor right now. Get dressed. Get your things."

"I don't know how he knew . . ."

"He went asking at the Empire, I'm told."

When Pender went out to sit with Father, Arch folded his clothes in a pile and rolled them into his canvas bag. Down the hallway, aware now of his father's murmuring voice, polite talk with Mr. and Mrs. Pender. When Arch came to the threshold of the room, his father smiled mildly, as if faintly amused.

"The prodigal son himself," Father said tersely. Arch knew enough to say nothing.

"We've been talking about you," Pender said.

Arch nodded.

"There's a place for you in the troupe, but not right now. Your father wants you to finish school."

Those words might as well have been a prison conviction. To be consigned back to a hardwood seat in a classroom, listening to the dronings of hard wooden people from whom he could learn nothing. He'd just begun to learn to fly! And now, grounded all over again.

ounterparts

HE IS A CHILD *again, playing in a broad and sunlit field. Without cares or pain, nearly floating on the air. He's running, and he kicks a ball, which thumps through the dew-wet grass. He is in a continuous moment of joy. He catches up with the ball and he kicks it again, hard, and it skitters off toward the margins. When he looks behind him, he sees, to his surprise, that no one is there.*

He stops. He is completely alone. He has the urge to call out, but then he doesn't. This is a pristine place, and a soundless one. Even the breeze is silent. He hears no birds. Blue sky and green fields, saturated with color and light.

Then he sees, beyond the ball, another person, standing just at the edge of the trees.

This figure barely stands out from the shrouded darkness of the thick woods. Archie, so curious, approaches. It is a boy, who does not move forward to meet him. Archie looks at him and sees what seems an image of himself. But this boy is pale, as if he's never once been in the light. He looks as alone in this world as Archie.

"Will you play with me?" the boy says.

"Who are you?"

"I'm John."

His dead brother. Long-lost. Long-forgotten. Never before met. But this is he, standing here with Arch, and just like himself. Archie can see this face as if his own in a mirror, but the face carries a deep sadness.

"Is this where you live?" Archie says from the sunshine.

"Yes."

"Are you lonely?"

"Yes."

"So am I."

"Do you want to play?"

"I was kicking the ball."

"But you can come with me and play."

"I don't know where that is."

"Will you come with me?"

"Where?"

The boy motions into the shadows.

"Come with me," he says.

"I don't know if I can."

"I'll take you to Mother," the boy says.

Arch looks into the darkness, but he can't see anything. The trees are thickly grown, so close-set they're like slats on a fence through which light cannot penetrate. High above, the canopies are so heavy that the leaves look black. Arch is out in the sun, under a blue sky, but all alone. He's at the edge of the light as his brother is at the edge of the shadows.

The boy recedes a step now, widening the space between them. "I can't stay. I need to go back. Come with me."

Arch is frozen, unable to choose. Behind him is brightness and *solitude; in front of him is the darkness of uncertainty, and possibility.*

1959

HE'S STARTING OUT THE working year in Key West, filming.
A war comedy, with a pink submarine, Tony Curtis, and any
number of beautiful young ladies. Joan O'Brien's breasts seem
to be co-starring, as the script is so resolutely built on that fact.
But it's easy money: He's taken an ownership stake up front and
seventy-five percent of the net profits on the back end; it's in his
interests for this to work out well. The minute he agreed to do
the film, the studio had increased the shooting budget from a
million dollars to three million.

But as they've begun the work, he's lost his enthusiasm. The
jokes seem suddenly stale. The premise is vacant. The young
director, Blake, seems just a bit too clever for his own good. The
women seem too young, and his disaffection is punctuated by
the opening scene, which was supposed to be nearly two decades
after the main events of the story.

They call him to makeup that morning of the scene, and the
makeup assistant, Donna, looks him over and says, "So we need
to make you old."

"Pardon?"

"We need to make you old, because it's in the script."

"How old?"

"Much older, actually."

"You don't say."

"The character is in his mid-fifties before the story flashes back."

"But I am in my mid-fifties."

"That's why it'll take some work. You look too young to be
that old."

"I suppose I should say I'm flattered."

"Nah. I didn't make it this way, I just need to fix it."

"So the opening of the picture is me looking old? That's the first thing they see, a preview of my decline?"

"That's what Blake wants."

"Well, I suppose I should have a word with Blake, then."

Blake, like most directors, is a charmer. He's always smiling as if he'd just been making fun of you behind your back. A joke, it seemed, was always in play. Donna leaves the makeup room, as if from one's dental chair as one awaits the drill. And a while later, Blake comes in, smiling without conviction.

"What's going on?"

"Let's talk outside."

So they go out into the morning sun and Blake takes out his cigarettes. He seems nervous beneath the smile. He says, "So what exactly is the problem?"

"See here, Blake, I don't know why we have to start that way," the Acrobat says. The Florida heat is surprising for winter; the bit of makeup already applied adds to the sense of his face burning. Blake considers this and says, "But you read the script. It was always this way."

"I read it indeed. If anything, start me off as I am and then make me younger. That would be an intriguing turn."

"Too much of a challenge," Blake says. "Your hair has no gray, you're not that wrinkled or saggy . . ."

"Thanks for that."

"You're certainly welcome. But anything else we try to do may be a bit . . . suspect. There's very little to work with. The problem is, you just look too good!"

"I'm as old as the script says I am and then you make me look twenty years older!"

Blake lets out a saddened sigh.

"Let's try to meet halfway," he says.

"Donna," he says as she works on him, "how did you get into this business, anyway?"

Donna is a woman seemingly of his own age, with a business-like manner and a seeming immunity to being impressed.

"Not much of a story. Started out in New York, doing theater makeup. Started hating winter, so Florida here I come. Down here, I still get work when a picture comes to town. I'm always happy for the work. This pays more than trying to make old Miami Beach ladies look younger."

"But I'd guess you get more gratitude."

"I'm not a time machine, so, let's say not always."

"But adding years isn't as hard?"

"Pretty easy, actually. A little gray here and there, some worry lines . . . But I'll keep it light. I'm not going to make you look like Spencer Tracy or anything."

"You know he's only four years older than me."

"Hard miles on him, then. I'll go easy."

"I am, I regret to say, your canvas."

"With a bit of time and some more supplies, I could make you unrecognizable."

"With a bit more time, I'll get there myself. The clock seems to run faster than when I was a boy."

"It only feels that way. But your clock isn't running as fast as some people I know."

"High praise, indeed."

"Did I hit a nerve, dear?"

"Not so much. I'd like to think I'll age with some grace and happiness."

"Attaboy," Donna says.

After the makeup's applied and the requisite scenes are shot, he sits alone in his dressing room and reflects upon his reflection, his older self, a sneak preview. Not terrible; don't we all when we're young contemplate our aged selves as one might a freak show: doddering and unkempt, flaccid, shaky? But at the age of fifty-five, he's none of those things and is determined never to be. His weight has stayed exactly at 180 pounds for decades; his tan seems so baked in as to never fade, and his hairline holds firm. His hair dark. His strong chin. No wattles or jowls. It is the makeup that serves to diminish him; he looks at himself in the mirror and sees what feels like victory, over the years of cigarettes and enthused drinking and quiet, hidden dissolution. Not bad, really.

The knock on the door sounds like a second one, as if the first was missed in his ruminations. The knob turns and in comes Blake, smiling as always.

"A moment?" he says.

"Indeed."

"I need for you to do something we're adding to the script."

"Let's hear it, then."

"We're going to have you steal a pig."

"For what purpose?"

"For the story—food. For the movie, laughs. For the splurch."

"Well, here's the problem. My characters don't steal, and won't be associated with a pig."

"So the gag is you dress the pig up like a human—like a drunken sailor—and cart it right by shore patrol and back to the sub. It will be hilarious."

The Acrobat stares at his older incarnation in the mirror, and sees someone too dignified to carry any pig. In his younger days, he'd have done it instantly, but as with a lot of things these days, he's not that man anymore.

"Well, I think not," he says.

"Oh, for crying out loud. It'll be the bit everybody remembers!"

"That's exactly what I'm afraid of."

"Which is why it's the perfect bit."

"Blake, let's just agree that we'll not."

The director suddenly drops to one knee, as if proposing marriage.

"I am sincerely begging you," he says. "Look, shoot the scene anyway. You own the film. You can get rid of the footage if you don't think it's any good. But just let us show you what we're talking about."

"It's not something I would ever do."

"But it's something the character would do. And we're talking about a character you play."

"Yes," the Acrobat says. "Well aware."

"But I thought we'd have some fun with this picture," Blake says.

"Dear boy, who ever told you that making a comedy is fun?"

"I wonder, Mr. Grant, do you find you prefer the Adler Method or the Strasberg Method?"

The Acrobat sits pondering this binary choice. The young woman doing the asking is one of the film's group of minor actresses, brought in to meet him before the shooting is under way. They're in a meeting room with a rattling air conditioner with the shades tight against the Florida sun. It's the fourth day of production, and the producer and friend Bob Arthur has the theory that a bit of meet-and-greet will allay nervousness on the set once their scenes begin shooting. They've gathered around the Acrobat in this room, which reminds him of a grammar school. The young women are all rising starlets with a chance to be noticed, and they know it. He's spoken briefly before entertaining questions, though he can barely remember what he's just said, or how to answer such a preposterous question. *The Method? On this picture?*

"I have no method at all, only madness," he says.

Only a smattering of giggles.

"But I really mean that, ladies. That's not the way we learned. What we do is not classical acting, either. It's studio acting. The gift to all of us is being given roles playing people we mostly are. Or who we wish we were. The better you do, the more they craft you these characters, like an outfit. Just slip it on and you're ready to shine. Now, it's not to say that I'm the same as Jimmy Stewart, but we're close enough to compete for the same roles. And there's always someone new, whom the studio tries to conform to what I do, which may allow them to fill a role at a lower cost but realize greater profit. I may have taken a few roles away from Ronald Colman for the same reason, once upon a time. It's a business, and we do our bit in it."

One of the actresses raises her hand, and he nods at her.

"How do you do better, though? What can we do right now?"

"I can tell you one secret I come back to again and again, if you'd like. Something you can all do right now, in this picture we're shooting."

As in all these instances, of course, they lean in, eager.

"You must listen."

He sees the usual looks of puzzlement.

"But we *are* listening," one says.

"No, no, *that's* the secret—listening."

"Listen when?" one says.

"Always, I'd say. But here I mean in your acting. Do think about it: It's a rare actor who spends as much effort in a scene listening, instead of simply waiting to speak. You think of your work as being heard. But imagine two actors who appear to simply be delivering alternating monologues. Or worse, an actor who mugs and displays while silent, upstaging the one doing the talking.

"It seems to me our audience has to believe that our characters actually care enough to listen. Listening, you see, is a very active thing. You listen and inside your own head, you think. Have you ever thought of how you're playing that?"

All the bright faces have lighted up.

"You've heard a line so many times in rehearsal, and read it so many times on the page, that it seems nothing more than a prompt anymore. So you have to then listen as if hearing it for the first time. I didn't say 'Act as if you're listening,' you see? Hear it, and when you hear it you might believe that other person is real and not an actor, and then you might believe you're real and not just an actor, but really living in that world."

They are sitting silently.

"Please don't share this secret too broadly," he says, cementing the bond of complicity.

Furious nods.

"And so far as the Method is concerned," he says, "I wonder how hard many of these actors work at the listening part. I'll give that Brando credit, he's one who does. The rest of them, I'm not so sure."

They're smiling, gratified, and he adds one more thing.

"We have an affliction as actors, don't we? We always want attention, onstage and off. It's our personalities, and our need. It's driven us far and wide, seeking it, and we often come to see it as our due. But do we hear? Are we listening as human beings?"

He thinks about where he's heading with it all but catches himself.

"You see right now? I've done nothing but talk, and I'm

talking about listening! But are there any other questions?"

A hesitant girl raises her hand.

"You don't cry in your pictures. Is that because you don't use the Method?"

"If you cry on screen, your audience won't cry. When you don't cry when you should, the audience cries for you. There's a difference between the theater and theatrics, don't you think?"

Silence. Bob Arthur, over on the side of the room, is smiling the producer's smile, seeing everyone coming together. Tony Curtis is supposed to arrive tonight, and the Acrobat knows that the ladies' attention will shift to him, once Curtis is on the set.

The Acrobat waits, but they all are in their seats smiling at him, as if seeing something they never thought was real. He remembers that feeling, when on that ship Fairbanks had looked at him and smiled.

"Anything else, then?"

One girl raises her hand, the beaming student.

"Is it true you can still do somersaults, even at your age?" she says.

That evening, Curtis's car brings him to the hotel. The Acrobat has been told he is the first person he wants to see. Yes, proper tribute to be made; Bob Arthur told him the young star was unwilling to give up top billing on the film to anyone but the Acrobat himself.

And, of course, he's seen Curtis in *Some Like It Hot* doing his pitch-perfect impression of the Acrobat himself. He hadn't been sure at the time if this was out of adulation or mockery, but it was spot on. He'd said to Bob Arthur, "This boy does a good me." Bob had said, "That's because he wants to be you."

When Curtis enters, avoiding the lobby by taking the kitchen entrance and then the service elevator, the Acrobat is alerted that he's on his way up. He stands by the door and when he hears the elevator bell issue its ding, he feels a small tensing. How this first moment works will have a lot to do with the success of the picture, and he already knows Curtis and Blake won't get along very well.

He presses his ear by the door and hears the shuffling footsteps. Then the soft knock. He counts silently to ten before opening the door. And there the man is, a glowingly handsome young fellow with a winning smile, his star ascendant. A young man like the Acrobat himself had been so long ago.

And this young man extends his hand for it to be shaken.

"Pleased to meet you," he says. "I'm Bernie Schwartz, from the Bronx, New York . . ."

The Acrobat grips his hand as well.

"Pleased to meet you as well," he says. "I'm Archie Leach, from Bristol, England . . ."

And they burst out with a laugh then, at exactly the same moment.

1920

THAT FIRST DAY, WHEN they disembarked the *Olympic* in New York, they got out of the taxis on Sixth Avenue at Forty-Third, and walked into the Hippodrome at ten in the morning. The New York Hippodrome dwarfed the Bristol Hippodrome by multiples. Arch could instantly feel himself afloat on shaky knees. They came through the stage door and he both marveled at, and understood, the dense mechanics of the place, as intricate as the workings of a fine pocket watch. Ropes and iron counterweights, rigging and catwalks and bank upon bank of electric lights. They came up onto the stage that seemed as large as a football pitch. It was a theater more cavernous than he could have imagined even existed.

"Five thousand three hundred seats," Pender said. "Five thousand three hundred people, watching you."

"When do we start?" Arch said.

"Tonight. So be ready. Same act, same work, same as always. Just a bigger stage. So we play it bigger."

On the way out, they wound back through the dimly lit backstage. Arch trailed behind, taking in everything. From down the way, a thumping sound, unfamiliar and its source unseen. Arch broke off a bit and in the darker reaches his eyes adjusted. And he made out glassy orbs shining back at him, too wide-set to be livestock. He stepped a bit closer and let his eyes further adjust. He realized he was looking at three elephants, looking back at him. They stood shifting lightly on chained hind legs, in their bed of straw. A voice beyond that: "Never seen one before?"

A small man, the presumed keeper, was leering at Arch from the shadows. The accent seemed local, an unknown and nasal variant of the mother tongue.

"Only in pictures."

"See this one here? Houdini made her disappear, right on stage."

"How did you ever get her back?"

The keeper gave Arch a long and uncertain stare. "Plenty to see. Show's at five, kid."

"I'm in the show, just like the elephants," Arch said.

Over the next days of rehearsals on the Hippodrome stage, Arch continued to be quietly daunted by the immensity of the place. During a break, he climbed the stairs to the cheap seats, up in the very farthest corner of the place. He looked down upon the stage and imagined how small he would look, how all his mugging and miming and broad gestures would yet be mostly lost to such distance. Who would ever notice him from such a vantage? The movies were so much bigger, even from the worst seats. Fairbanks and Pickford would look like Lady Liberty if projected in this cavern. So he knew how much bigger he'd really need to be.

At night, in their room of four in their cheap hotel, Arch watched Billy sit at the open window, watching the street scene. The thousands below, and the tens of thousands beyond. Billy hadn't spoken again of his planned defection, but there was no doubt it remained fully in play.

And then, after the rehearsals and before the performances began, a Sunday off. Very early that morning, despite Pender's admonitions to stay within two blocks of the hotel, Arch set off alone for Coney Island. At Second Avenue, he took a downtown train at Canal Street, then switched to the Brighton Beach Line on the advice of a man on the platform who seemed to know what he was talking about. Arch was overdressed, his woolen British clothes too heavy on a humid New York day. But he was exploring the city as if he'd never leave it, although he was not yet admitting his intrigue with Billy's plan. The train was packed, making the air even closer; he perspired liberally. He'd shed his coat and would shed his shirt once there, anyway: time to turn his pale mien into the bronze of a Fairbanks.

The train trundled into the Stillwell Avenue Terminal. The doors opened and the crowd surged out in the direction of the boardwalk. He followed the swarm across Surf Avenue. To his left he could see the Wonder Wheel, the newly opened marvel. It turned slowly, like a spinning galaxy God had made from the ribs of the Eiffel Tower. To the right of that, the peaks and valleys of the Giant Racer roller coaster stood in the distance, a scaffolded mountain range. He smelled cinnamon, and fish, and cigarette smoke, all commingling in the humid air. The crowd around him seemed to rise in their animation, the voices louder and the cries of excitement an octave higher. Up the ramp onto the boardwalk itself, and then the glint of ocean. He had arrived. He was in the midst of a bright carnival far different than the musty theaters and overcast lanes of Bristol, as much as he had loved them. The seaside towns of Britain where the Pender Troupe had played were never as crowded as here, nor as warm. He could feel the high late-morning sun already cooking his forehead. He nervously took his money from his pocket and re-counted it, wanting to be sure he'd make it home. He had more than enough; it just never felt that way.

And for the next two hours, he just walked, looking at the crowd. He studied their faces, listening to their voices and absorbing their accents, the nuances of inflection and emphasis. He tried quietly repeating some of what he heard. He might have appeared, to a passerby, to be a young man quietly muttering to himself. But this was the beginning of an education.

Americans, at least on Coney Island, seemed more exuberant in their manners, and rougher. The restraint he'd observed on Fifth Avenue was cast aside over here by the ocean. From the subway egress, filled with shoves and elbows, and on the boardwalk, with few giving up space in their paths. He wove around, mostly. On the boardwalk, the ladies with their parasols smiled widely, even a few fluttering at him as he passed. In the water, thousands of people in swimming costumes stood shoulder-to-shoulder, with hardly room to move. Some of the men were bare-chested in the water, this display not apparently as scandalous as back in Britain.

Overheated, he found a bench facing the sun and removed his coat, tie, and shirt. Only his undervest separated him from barbarism. And, squared against the sun, he began what he imagined was transformation. The first step was to lose the wan pallor of his provenance. His time with the Pender Troupe, along with the inevitable maturation of adolescence, had made his arms sinewy, the musculature of a grown man.

He closed his eyes and stretched his right arm out on the bench, but his left stayed firmly in his pocket, clutching his money. It was the entirety of his wealth, folded into a small cylinder, and tightly gripped. He took it out and looked at it, then pocketed it again before he felt able to close his eyes and relax.

America. It was nearly fantasy, laid out in front of him. He listened to the crowds and the roar of surf, but then he felt the shadow of a cloud rolling across his face.

He opened his eyes. It wasn't a cloud, it was a girl, eclipsing the summer sun and presenting only as a dark silhouette before him. She wore a white flowered dress and a wide hat and as his eyes adjusted he could see she was smiling, and pretty.

"Aren't you just a peach," she said.

"You don't say," he answered, though he knew full well he was.

"When you get hair on your chest, you'll really be something."

His smile faltered briefly.

"I'm just teasing. Is anyone else sitting on the bench?"

When he didn't understand, she said, "May I sit down?"

He nodded, and she sat. He couldn't tell if she wanted to sit on the bench or sit with him, but then she said, "Your name, then?"

"Archie."

"Where are you from?"

"Around here."

"Where around here?"

"Manhattan."

"You sound like you're from somewhere else."

"Like where?"

"I don't know, Boston or something. Have I guessed it?"

"You're very perceptive."

"And you sound like you're a person of substance . . ."

"Oh, very much so. We often speak of that when we gather in the drawing room."

The girl smiled at that. He wasn't quite sure if she got the joke, and now he'd feel bad to explain. She said, "I'd be happy to show you around."

"Around where?"

"Around anywhere you want, handsome."

Americans, indeed! He stood to put his shirt back on, and buttoned it up as she watched.

"Let's go this way," she said. She took his arm and led him eastward, the sun behind them now and the salt breeze in their faces.

"Brighton Beach is in this direction," she said.

"I haven't asked your name."

"No," she said, "you haven't."

He waited and she didn't offer.

They walked on. He felt the rising thrill of an assured flirtation. He was already appreciating the frankness of these American girls.

"I've never been to Boston," the girl said. "What's it like?"

"In my neighborhood, rather deluxe. Only the finest people."

"What neighborhood is that?"

"Oh, I don't want to boast about it! And now tell me about Brighton Beach."

"Not so deluxe. Just people, living their lives. People getting by. We're not as well-to-do as you, Arch."

"Some of us are more fortunate than others. I often say that to our man, Melvyn."

"Your man?"

"Yes, our *majordome*, if you will. Ours was a large place and you could always find him at the door. *Gardien de la maison*, he called himself. Our place was called the Empire."

"Sounds quite grand. So you live the high life, then."

"Oh, I don't know about that! But I was saying to Fairbanks and Pickford that I do enjoy traveling."

"Fairbanks and Pickford?"

"Oh, yes. Playing a bit of shuffleboard on the way over. On the *Olympic*. I was just over in England, you see . . ."

The ease with which he was recasting himself was revelatory. But he knew he couldn't see this girl again, lest he be found out. Thus it would be a fleeting interlude. But the more he spun his nearly-true falsities, the more full of himself he felt. His face would be sunburned tonight, he could feel it already. But in the days after the tan would emerge, the beginning of a metamorphosis to worldliness and self-possession.

She turned toward him now and looked hard in his eyes.

"I'm not going to tell you my name yet," she said, "but I'll show you something. If we go underneath the boardwalk, no one will be able to see us."

"Why would we want that?"

She smiled, coyly, and then he understood. To steal a kiss, maybe. Something more, maybe. He followed her down the wooden steps to the sand, and then turned with her to go underneath. Even on this bright day, the underside of the boardwalk was a shadowed expanse. Even as his eyes adjusted, he could only distinguish the basic shapes, the forest of pilings, and the slivers of sunlight that had snuck through the spaces between the boards.

She took him by the hand and led him toward the darkness. Her hands were small, and in the heat of the day her palms were moist. He was walking into an unknown, the secrets of women he would have loudly sworn he knew but had not fully absorbed. He was excited; he was terrified. He was already convincing himself that this eventuality itself—of a girl pulling him into dark intimacies—was a victory already.

"Wait," he said, tightening on her hand and stopping her progress.

She turned, and in the dark, he couldn't read her face.

"Let's go back up," he said, stepping away a few feet.

"Don't be such a spoilsport," she said.

"Oh, I'm not at all." He was now exerting more of a pull on her, moving her back toward the light. "In fact, I'd like to do this properly . . ."

She yanked her sweaty hand from his grip and stepped back into the shadows.

"Do *what* properly?"

"A date."

She seemed to be collecting herself. "You're on a proper date right now," she said.

"We both know that's not quite the case. At least where I come from."

"It's true on Coney Island," she said.

"I suppose I'll need to get used to Coney Island, then."

"Come with me now or don't bother me," she said, her voice curdling.

"That seems awfully harsh." But he was already hearing that hard side of her he could recall in his mother, that tarnished backside of the shiny coin. He continued to back away.

"Are you really throwing me over?" she said. As she advanced, following him back toward the sun, he could see the fiery glint in her eyes, like a feral animal ready to pounce.

"I can't be. We only just met."

"Do you think you're too good for me now?"

"Quite the opposite!"

This moment was over. He was out on the hot sand and moving toward the stairway and she stood at the edge of the shadows, her face a mask of fury. And then, behind her, a man stepped out from the dark where he had been hiding, and stood beside her, with a look Arch would remember later as truly menacing. This man was much older and much larger than Arch. He was in his undershirt, his skin slick from sweating in the heat in the airless depths beneath the footsteps treading above.

"Come on back here, rich boy, I have something for you," the man said, the taunt of someone who had just lost the game. Then the man glared at the girl, who looked downward to avoid his scrutiny, the wide brim of her hat eclipsing a face he would forget in a very short time.

"Not on your bloody life!" Arch called back, and he was fully, flatly, breaking into a run.

The World as One Finds It

IT'S A TIME OR *a place or a universe (he's not sure) in which manners do not exist. It is a reality peopled by a genus that has developed a brain that does not process such abstractions. Courtesy, refinement, and that most ethereal quality of all—class—are not known or even understood. Directness is the currency. Vulgarity, ugliness, and anger are on full display. But so are happiness, joy, and sentimentality. And love. This world has not learned the skill of concealment or circumspection, cannot read gesture and discretion.*

In this existence, there is nothing held back. Like children who have not been taught to control their impulses, its leaders rail and condemn, and their followers rage and lash out. On the streets, people shove by each other, because each does not hold any immediate value or utility to another. In the home, family members say whatever they want the moment they feel it, without regard to the longer damage. But they also empty their hearts in no uncertain terms. Trust is a little-known state of mind, as the subtle signals of such high-function thinking go unprocessed by underdeveloped frontal lobes that are the trait of this species. But without trust there is not expectation, and without expectation there is not disappointment. These greater calculations are nuances that seem preposterously overcomplicated.

He, with his aberrant pathology, is an outlier, gifted with qualities and talents for which there is no practical use. His discomfort at speaking his mind is diagnosed as a mental defect. His withholding of blunt statement is understood to be a disability. His quips elicit only blank countenance. They're seen as dangerous diversion. He hides from those who would abuse him for it, and when he walks in the world, he conceals any behavior that might signal it.

There's little humor in a world where the abstractions of a joke are lost on most. There's no room for irony or suggestiveness. The only entertainment for the masses is made of the most blunt forces to be mustered: Belittlement. Mockery. Retribution. Direct, unvarnished attack is the order of the day.

But this world somehow functions, nonetheless. People get up in the morning, go to work, come home to their families. From a distance, nothing may seem amiss, because what is missing is so subtle. What is missing is a social conceit that in other worlds seems essential.

But here and there, he detects people who seem to understand, and seem, possibly, to be like him. They'll never admit it, for fear of being outcasts. But in the shadows, they can read each other's signals. Like a sixth sense. And while the people of this world would not even comprehend it, those with this subtle talent appreciate it in others, and feel less alone. And in their talent for withholding, for deflection, and for subtlety. They make a small subculture where someone can feel insulated, even protected. Only those similarly afflicted can see what is the better part of him.

1922

AFTER THAT FIRST RUN in New York City, the Pender Troupe turned westward. On to the vaudeville circuit. Across the American Midwest, shows in St. Louis, Cleveland, Milwaukee, and town after small town between. Train rides sleeping sitting up, and then coming into a town at dawn; napping in the seats of the empty theater before shows, then performing and eating and then back on the train. Some layovers in cheap hotels where the sleep debt was repaid in full, sometimes sprawled on beds fully clothed. Arch was in the heart of America but felt as if he'd never truly been there, only seeing it from the window of a train.

Part of the act was a dancing cow in which Arch occupied the back end of the heavy canvas costume. He and Sammy Curtis, who was all of four feet seven, did a bit called "The Long and the Short of It." Pender was always adding something, subtracting something, and using the American laughs as his calibration.

In the bigger cities of the middle of America, he'd see double lines queued outside the theater, the white and the black; when the curtain rolled back and smiled into the light, he could see the white faces before him and the black faces in the balconies far above. He'd had no experience with all this in lily-white England, and hardly knew what to make of it, other than to think that he and his castmates just wanted to make everyone smile. It seemed the simplest philosophy he could conjure.

In his time in America, Arch had grown up. He'd turned eighteen in January 1922, something that escaped anyone's notice because he'd been acting as if he was eighteen since he was fourteen. But now in June of that year, back in New York City, he and Billy sat in Pender's hotel room and said they were taking their chances in America. It didn't seem to be taken as a surprise.

"Let me give you your return fare," Pender said. "We'll start rehearsals in September for the winter season back home."

The money, fifty-five dollars for a third-class berth, was substantial. Pender wrapped his arms around Arch and gave him a tight hug, and then Billy, who seemed to tighten in his embrace.

"Have your adventure, boys, and then come home safe to us," he said.

He and Billy went back to their room to pack. Checkout time was noon and they weren't at all sure what came next.

Arch sat on the bed and wondered if he'd made a huge mistake. He also tried to imagine what his father would have to say upon his nonreturn. But neither could he truly conclude he'd be missed by the man. Like his mother, Arch had now made his exit. He was in a hotel room in New York, and safe. He wasn't poor doomed Charnley on a troop ship, with the trenches and cannons and poison gas up ahead. Arch was just in show business, a far-lower-stakes war that nonetheless made people into clear winners or losers.

"No time to slouch around now," Billy said, but Arch could see that Billy was churning with anxiety as his year-and-a-half-long plan had finally come to bear. "We need to sort out how to bloody make this work."

With their ticket money closely guarded, they found shelter with new friends, squatting with other young actors they'd known from the backstage of the Hippodrome, and who'd similarly taken those vows of poverty for the riches of the spotlight's glare. But, as yet, their performances were impromptu and afield of the familiar boards.

Arch began to make money instantly. Stilt-walking was a lifesaver, as it turned out. Arch landed jobs for advertisers and promoters; he'd navigate the wide Manhattan sidewalks handing out leaflets and learning to watch for the malicious kick meant to take him down. The auditions had been easy: The stilts were only three-footers, made of ash, the likes of which he hadn't worn since he was a Pender novice; he was rock-solid against any assaults.

Billy, meanwhile, was being paid a pittance to be an audience plant for some magicians, dragged to the stage but prepped on the illusion. On off nights, the two of them walked Times Square in sandwich boards promoting various bars and theaters. For recreation, they did more of the same. They sang on park benches and shuffled decks of cards endlessly. They were tumblers, so they tumbled. A hat put out for coins reaped them small royalties. They congratulated themselves on tricking the world in so many ways.

Falling down stairs started out as a lark. They bragged about falling down some of the finest staircases in New York City. The grand staircase of the Ritz-Carlton. The much-trickier Criterion Theatre on Broadway at Forty-Fourth Street, with a wide landing before a second set of stairs. They tumbled down steep aisles at the Polo Grounds, where Arch's first glimpse of baseball enthralled him, with its Americanness.

They'd been taught by Pender how to fall without injury or risk; staircases were child's play compared to the troupe's more elaborate demonstrations. It was just the youthful urge to display their talents, whether people wanted to see them or not. Each tumble was a set piece, with some small plot. Sometimes they waited for pretty girls to be unsuspecting audiences, just to watch them smile and blush. Sometimes they added a bit of fun by beginning the process by bumping into some unsuspecting gent, as if that had caused the accident. It shook up a few men, and most were amused in the aftermath.

Then, one day with Billy, he tumbled down the stairs at the Biltmore. The truly grand hotels had stairways so thickly carpeted Arch felt as if he were a child somersaulting down a grassy hill, though he still registered the gasps and cries around him. He was utterly convincing. The Biltmore's main staircase had eight and then seven steps, separated by a landing. The trick on these stairs was that at the midway landing, he pulled himself up and pantomimed wobbling knees and spinning head before taking that next errant step to pitch himself down the lower set of stairs. It was his habit of making the final flourish of playing dead, if just for a moment, before springing up with a smile and a bow. It was all a matter of honed timing, but today he found himself at the bottom, and perhaps waiting a tick too long before rising.

He'd barely brushed the white-mustached man at the top of the stairs, but that had set the fall in motion. As he rose to his feet the man came rushing down the stairs.

"Good God, are you all right, boy?" the man said.

"Well, that was a bloody muddle," Arch said in his Fairbanks voice. "Just a small loss of equilibrium, and downwardly I went."

"You must be in terrible pain!"

"Well, I most certainly might be . . ."

"Is anything broken?"

"I'd say I can't say." And Billy hovering just behind a pillar, grinning madly.

The man was shoving a ten-dollar bill into Arch's hand.

"Take this and see a doctor," he said. "Make sure you're well!"

Arch was speechless. But . . . ten dollars! He and Billy went down to the Childs Restaurant on Cortlandt Street, where the fish cakes were twenty cents and boiled eggs ten cents. Even eating their fill, there was plenty of money left over, an unexpected and laughable windfall. Billy was already thinking about that, and how soon enough they would be very hungry again.

Soon enough, then, Billy made the staircases of Manhattan his primary performing venue. Arch went along with him the first few times. Billy would wait for a well-appointed gentleman to come down the chosen staircase, typically a man with his attention on his watch, or a newspaper, or his own thoughts. Billy would then step into that man as if accidentally, but harder, to make it feel real. Then he would go falling down the stairs. Arch had to admire the showmanship, for Billy's marks believed, undoubtingly, they had caused this boy's terrible accident. And Billy could sincerely act hurt, pushing himself up from the floor as if on the verge of cranial bleeding.

"I'd see a doctor if I had any money," he'd wheeze, as the worried man shoved cash into his hand. It was rarely a tenner, but it all added up. Arch sometimes took the fall, but it was in those instances Billy who would play the shocked bystander, guilting the day's marked man into forking over some doctor money. Arch refused to make the ask.

The act was highly portable, not limited to hotel lobbies. He could pick the stairs at the City Hall subway station, or the grand hall at the Metropolitan Museum of Art, or the bridges of Central Park. It had become Billy's primary source of income, as he struggled to find anything else that paid as well.

But Arch had begun to find reasons not to join in; the joke had gotten a little tired. And while Arch could not completely take the high ground, given his own forgeries and fibs on the way to the theater, Billy had committed an inviolable sin: It was no longer about the show.

One day, with Billy feeling the need for a payday, and insistent that Arch join him and do his bit, they were back at the Biltmore.

On this autumn Saturday afternoon, Arch sauntered along

the banister, assessing the possibilities. Up the stairs came a middle-aged man and his finely dressed wife, clearly of wealth and absorbed in their conversation. When Arch came by, the man didn't even try to slip past. Arch was not inclined to defer. Their shoulders hit with convincing force. And down he went.

The sensation of tumbling was always the truest pleasure. He'd become adept at surveying the path (he didn't want to sweep over some unsuspecting bystander) and enjoying the feeling of invulnerability. His talent was his armor. He'd caught Billy, after some of his falls, or rubbing an elbow or walking with the slightest limp. The signs of imperfect technique. So that became the competition in itself.

Falling, this time, he was dreaming of fish cakes and boiled eggs. And soon enough, he arrived at the finish, sprawling onto the lobby at the foot of the stairs.

But hands were on him, pulling him up, and behind the man in the bellhop suit was another man who appeared to be the concierge, dark suit and paintbrush mustache, looking quite alarmed.

"Are you hurt, young man?" the concierge nearly shouted.

"I think I'll be all right."

"Well, gather yourself. I'm here for you, sir."

The couple he had bumped, he realized, were not coming down the stairs. He wondered if the woman had encouraged the man to keep walking. Billy had shrunk out of sight.

They stood until the people who had witnessed his fall had dispersed. The lobby resumed its business. The concierge now led him by the elbow to the hotel entrance and onto Forty-Third Street.

"Be sure you're well," the concierge said. "And good God, man, stay away from that staircase." Then he clenched Arch's arm much too tightly, and he spoke in a rougher voice laced with Brooklynese.

"You better avoid the Biltmore altogether, if you get what I'm saying."

Billy met Arch outside.

"Well, you mucked that one up," Billy said. "What happened?"

"It went perfectly. But the man didn't come to see if I was all right."

"Then you picked the wrong man!"

"Maybe so. But he was with his wife, and I was sure he'd try to be gallant."

"It probably wasn't his wife, Arch."

"Yes, never thought of that."

Billy shook his head. "What are we going to do about food? Shall we try another hotel? The Commodore, maybe?"

"I've lost my appetite," Arch said.

Billy was the very last connection to England, no small thing. Arch was working up to the next step, but he found himself attached to Billy out of their shared dare to stay on. On a particular Saturday afternoon months later, they entered the Biltmore's lobby once again. Billy, in his suit and tie and polished shoes, took his place at the top of the marble-and-bronze staircase. He'd become tired, he said, of second-rate hotels with small payouts. Winter had set in and work was scarce. Billy said he was always hungry.

Arch, not wanting to be spotted, edged behind a tall potted fern in the lobby. He was only there at Billy's behest, and ready to decamp, once a bit of food money had been procured.

And at the top of the stairway, a scream, and Billy cartwheeling hard down the steps. Four people came running down toward him, the poor injured boy. At the bottom, he lay crumpled in a fair impression of a broken leg as other guests rushed over.

Arch reflexively stepped back, and bumped against something.

And the vise of a familiar hand tightening on his bicep.

"Why, that fellow is as uncoordinated as you are, my young friend."

Arch had not actually done anything, but he suspected that didn't much matter.

"Now, young fellow, I urged you once before, for your well-being, to avoid the Biltmore. Yet you've returned. And who could forget such a handsome face? Do you have a room here at the hotel?"

"I don't even know that boy," Arch said.

"And who said you did? You're answering questions nobody's asked you."

Over at the bottom of the stairs, two men were clearing the crowd. One, a bearded man in a bowler, went to one knee and whispered into Billy's ear. Billy sprang up, instantly, as the onlookers startled at his instantaneous recovery. But the men had their hands on him and they looked over to Arch.

"Let's get them both in my office," the concierge said.

"What do I have to do with any of this?" Arch said, and Billy flashed him the Judas look.

"Part of the scheme, I'd think," the bearded man said.

In the office, Arch and Billy avoided any eye contact with each other. It was a long interlude. The bearded man in the bowler was a hotel detective. Eventually, the concierge had come in and spoken of the misfortune that would meet them if they came within a block of the hotel, ever again. "Part of my job is to remember every face," he said. "But you know that now, don't you?"

And after they'd been warned and released, they walked back to their shared room not speaking.

"I think it's time to go back to England," Billy finally said. "We're not even getting enough to eat."

"Suits me just fine to stay on," Arch said. "So good luck with it all."

"But I don't have any money to get back."

"Well, I'll need to leave you to all that, Billy, and bid you goodbye now." And he began to pack, not even sure where he was going next.

That was the end of that. Arch in his youth and ambition, out the door, erasing Billy from his mind nearly instantly, only to wonder about him years later, then eventually forget all about him again. Billy had been swept up by the magic of the stage but had suffered the worst fate of all: to be talentless in things that turned out to matter.

1959

HE'S FOUND A SPOT in the sun on the deck of a pink submarine, and he's awaiting the dull pain of being interviewed. He's never been one for press events, but they're a necessary evil.

The submarine, roped up to a dock at the Key West naval station, is a 311-foot Balao-class vessel that the studio has leased for the film. Its pink paint is in keeping with the somewhat tortuous plotline: During the war, a gaggle of nurses must join the crew; the sub, painted with a mixture of the only available primer—red and white—but not yet covered in its black outer coat, must set to its mission. The pink seems a bit much, the Acrobat thinks, but it goes perfectly with Blake's comic urges as a director: The man seems enamored with pink. "This Eastmancolor film stock will *love* it," he said in one of the production meetings.

The narrow deck has been rigged with handrails and a gangway and a set of studio chairs, so that the interviews may be conducted upon this, the film's most central and ostentatious

93

prop. Reporters love that sort of thing. The Acrobat has set himself up in the sun to get some color while he can. The other chairs, set up by the publicity people, remain in the cool of the shade behind the conning tower.

It's a brilliant tropical-winter day. A few reporters are coming from cold-weather cities, with the more-familiar Hollywood columnists at the end. The Acrobat steadies himself for churning out repeated answers to repeated questions; as with every picture, he will say this is likely the finest picture with which he's ever been associated. Hardly so; but he does feel certain the film will turn a profit. He's less sure about the film he recently completed with Hitch, tentatively titled *In a Northwesterly Direction*, involving a man on the run because of a mistaken identity. Today he'll be an affable liar. But lies in support of a picture are fair play, indeed.

The first reporter is brought out, another in a line the studio's promotion department has arranged. A nervous young woman from a Midwestern newspaper. She's apparently paid her way down on a midwinter vacation built around this interview, and has undoubtedly spent the morning grooming herself. She's short, with reddish hair tied back against the sea breeze, with cat-eye sunglasses and bright-red lipstick.

The publicist makes introductions: Doris Somebody from the Such-and-Such *Register*. It all goes by him, as they seat themselves. Facing the sun, he sees her through his Ray-Bans as a dark form in bright light, just a voice piping with questions that he's answered a thousand times before. Why is she here? Is a standard interview with an actor a plum assignment back at the *Register*? Nearly on automatic, he goes on and on about the delightful film he is engaged in, the rising co-star Tony Curtis and what a fine young actor he is. But he realizes he's saying it so blandly that he could be taken to be lying, which is untrue. The interview ends with the young woman shakily thanking him, as if she might begin to cry.

More of the same ensues: journalists from the local Miami papers, from Chicago, from Boston. An hour into it, a short break. Time for a glass of water. The publicist, a wiry man named James (last name or first remains unclear), who's been flown out by Ed Muhl at Universal, takes the seat closest to him.

"We should talk about the next interview," James says. "This one might be a little different."

"Why? Who is it?"

"Do you know Joe Hyams? Hollywood correspondent for the *New York Herald Tribune*?"

"Sure, I know Joe. At least enough to say hello. What about him?"

"You may know he was a war hero. Parachuted into combat in the Battle of Saipan. Wounded, medals for bravery, that kind of thing."

"And what does that have to do with me?"

"Just . . . this is a war picture."

"It's a comedy."

"Some of these men who actually fought, sometimes they resent guys who didn't fight . . ."

"I take your point, James."

"I'm just making you aware."

"If only war heroes got to play war heroes, Jimmy Stewart would be the only one making war movies," the Acrobat said.

"Hyams is a black belt in karate . . ."

"Well, he certainly makes Duke Wayne look silly, but I'm hardly purporting to be a war hero or an expert in karate. Did Hyams suggest he was feeling this way about me?"

"No. Mr. Muhl thought it best to be careful, given, well . . ."

"Well what?"

"That you spent the war in Bel Air with the richest woman in the world . . ."

"*One* of the richest. Please don't exaggerate."

". . . while this guy was dropping by parachute into machine-gun fire. He left Harvard to enlist."

"So he's everything people like me only pretend to be, is that it? But that's what we do, in the pictures, isn't it? I've never claimed to be anybody's hero."

"I'm not suggesting there will be a problem. In fact, Humphrey Bogart loved this guy."

"God rest Bogey's soul. But is that meant to be an endorsement?"

James says nothing.

"I suppose my lack of a war record will always be a nuisance," the Acrobat says. "But I was too young for one war, and too old for the other. And I did plenty helping the cause, as I could. I received the bloody King's Medal!"

"No one is suggesting you didn't," James says.

"Why, what did you do in the war, James?"

"I was at Salerno with the Fifth Army."

"All right, then, all right. So what do you want me to do?"

"Keep it light. Keep it chatty. Mr. Muhl just wanted you forewarned."

Hyams shows up on time and is brought over by James. As they come down the dock, Hyams is smiling broadly as he looks at the submarine. The man somehow looks bigger now than the Acrobat remembers him, and coming up the gangway he smiles as he extends his hand.

"Well, get a load of this sub," he says. "Is this supposed to be some kind of phallic symbol?"

"I personally like to think of mine as a rocket ship."

The reporter slowly grins.

"I guess we all need to feel strong, right?" he says.

Hyams has brought a small tape recorder, which he sets up on his lap. He holds the microphone in his left hand and lays his notepad on his right leg.

They seat themselves and James says, "I really don't think anyone had a phallic symbol in mind."

"But Freud would tell you that's how it works," the Acrobat says. "Fortunately or unfortunately, Mr. Hyams, I didn't write the script. You'll have to take it up with Blake. I think he knows exactly what he's doing."

"Fair enough," Hyams says, "but let's talk about you, then."

"Well, now I feel as if I should be lying on a couch."

"I've got nothing that probing. But wondering why, after some of your history, you've chosen this film."

"Why, what's wrong with this?"

"Nothing at all."

"So, by my history, you mean what?"

"Your recent roles. You've done *To Catch a Thief, An Affair to Remember*, and *Indiscreet* in the last few years. These set a certain tone, it seems. This seems a departure from the debonair socialite you're more accustomed to being."

"Well, the fact is that Tony Curtis wanted me to do this picture with him, and I wanted to. And truth to tell, I'm really no more a 'debonair socialite' than I was a submarine commander."

Hyams smiles again. "Is that so?"

"More than you know."

"Weren't you married to Barbara Hutton?"

James leans forward now and says, "His marriages are out of bounds, Joe."

Hyams nods. "It just seems debonair and social to me."

"I suppose that's the actor's craft, isn't it? For example, I recollect hearing that you were friendly with Bogey—God rest his soul—weren't you?"

"That's right."

"So there's the inversion. Son of a prominent surgeon, raised in New York City society. At the age I was stilt-walking on Coney Island, Bogey was attending an elite preparatory school. But everyone thought of him as a working-class tough case, because of the roles he played and made his own. That's a credit to the man, mind you."

Hyams is looking at him, but inscrutably so. Just a smiling man with an open face and no apparent malice.

"So," Hyams says, "this is a light comedy, which suits you."

"What do you mean by that?"

Hyams looks up, as if not sure how to proceed.

"It's what you do best, I'd think. You've made a life of these kinds of movies."

"Yes, a life trying to entertain people. It's what I do."

"It sounds like it's been a very good life."

"Again, it may seem that way," the Acrobat says, "but it's a complicated life, just like with most people. I've finally been delving into the reality of my life."

"Really. How so?"

"I've been born again."

"You've gotten religion?" Hyams says, writing furiously on his pad.

"No, nothing that extreme! No, I've been involved in psychotherapy, aided by a wonderful medication."

"What medication is that?"

"It's called LSD, actually. Have you heard of that?"

Hyams looks up at him, then looks down at his tape recorder to be sure it's running.

"I have indeed. Doesn't the military use it as truth serum?"

"Why, Joe, you look perfectly aghast. Or at least agape."

"I'm not judging. But please go on."

"I have been through a psychiatric experience which has completely changed me. It was horrendous. I had to face things about myself which I never admitted, which I didn't know were there. Now I know that I hurt every woman I ever loved. I was an utter fake, a self-opinionated bore, a know-it-all who knew little."

James has tightened in his chair and leans forward to intone, but the Acrobat waves him off and says, "We're just having a conversation."

"That's all very fascinating," Hyams says.

"Yes, it is. I found I was hiding behind all kinds of defenses and vanities. I had to get rid of them layer by layer. The moment when your conscious meets your subconscious is a hell of a wrench.

"Each of us is dying for affection, but we don't know how to go about getting it. Everything we do is affected by this longing. That's why I became an actor. I was longing for affection. I wanted people to like me, but I went about it in the wrong way. Most people do."

"But everybody loves you," Hyams says. "They always have."

"Which is why we should get back to discussing the picture," James says, weakly.

"You see, Mr. Hyams, my attitude toward women is completely different. I don't intend to foul up any more lives. I'm aware of my fault. I'm ready to accept responsibility."

"How does a person do that?"

"I know that a man and a woman deliberately spoil something that is beautiful between them. We cannot stop hurting ourselves and each other by destroying the one thing we're all dying for: love and affection."

Hyams looks at the little left of the unspooling tape and

shuts off the machine.

"May I publish what you just said?" he says.

"Oh, no, not yet," the Acrobat says. "I'll let you know."

To James's relief, Hyams turns the machine back on and says, "So tell me about this movie I'm here to learn about." And with that, the Acrobat loops back the answers he's already given the other reporters.

At the end of it all, Hyams stands and they shake hands, and waves a farewell as he goes down the gangway.

James looks at his notes. "Lionel Crane of the London *Daily Mirror*."

"Splendid. I know Lionel. He lives in Los Angeles, actually."

"Sir, if I may," James says, voice quivering, "perhaps best to not delve into personal history."

"Oh, that was all just chatting," the Acrobat says. "And it's not as if I'm ashamed, anyway. Why should I be?"

Towering

an

HE'S LOOKING DOWN ON *the crowd, astride what seem the longest stilts he's ever mastered. He gazes upon the heads of his fellow men, who likewise look up at him in awe. The people beneath him part as he passes. Some of them reach up to try to touch his hand.*

But he's too tall to meet their outstretched fingers. Even bending as far as he can, he cannot make that basic contact, as much as he tries to, and wants to. He smiles instead, and waves, and amazes them with a deep bow that is a picture of perfect balance. It is a show he loves to give, to amuse and to surprise. He is, after all, a showman. He walks the streets, soaking up the attention. And when he looks up from the people, he is closer to the sky; his vistas are spread farther than anyone down below could imagine seeing.

But at day's end he is ready to dismount his stilts; when he reaches to unstrap them, he feels nothing but flesh and bone. There is no wood and leather. These are his legs, as if the stilts have grafted themselves to him. He can't remove them. And he's not sure he wants to. It's a thrill to loom so far above the masses, to be seen and to be admired. He is set apart. To leave his lofty perch is to return to the anonymity that most people occupy below.

And when the days end, and he finds his way back to a home as grand as his stature, the aloneness sets in, as much as he fights it. In his chair, looking at his endless legs reaching out before him, the towering man fights that sense that he has separated himself from the very simple pleasures the small people revel in. He imagines a group of them, gathered in some cozy place, one of them sharing the story of having seen this glorious man and having marveled at what a sight it was.

He thinks of Gulliver on his travels, frightening and mighty. He imagines the Lilliputians as swarms and not as discrete beings, as we all are. But as with Lemuel Gulliver, the towering man understands not only the awe at him but also the fear of him, the suspicion, and the stories told that may be as fantastical as their worries. But he recalls that first step onto a low pair of stilts, and then the struggle to the next-highest, and upward until it is natural that his growth has ascended to a height from which he cannot any longer step down.

1924

THE AFTER-SHOW GATHERINGS always began deep in the night, after the stages had been cleared, the theater makeup scoured from sweated faces, wardrobes reracked, and the excitement let to dissipate. Sleep was always still far away. The exit from a dark theater into the quiet streets could still not calm enlivened minds, and in many predawns, as this one, word was general as to where one should go to find kindred souls. On this early-spring evening everyone was restless; too much winter and now the prospect of a summer with the shows closed.

The party was at a garden apartment somewhere in the Village, in a narrow building that seemed mostly peopled by performers. Arch arrived with two boys with whom he'd been cast in a short-run slapstick, in a tiny theater; he knew them as Russ and Leo, and doubted he'd know them after the show ended. But here they all were, plunging into body heat and noise. The room was a chamber of peeling wallpaper and weak-bulbed lamps and a mantel lined with burned-down candles. Chairs and two worn-out sofas were pushed up against the walls. A Victrola in the corner was clearly the only expensive piece of furniture in the place. The record that was playing was "Paddlin' Madelin' Home," by Ukulele Ike. Some girls were dancing with each other. They were all flappers this year; not Arch's style, but times were changing, even when you were twenty. The girls were loud and opinionated and usually drunk, and that made things lively.

"I'm getting a drink," Russ said, and Arch followed to the bottles lined up on a wide windowsill. The liquor had been pre-diluted by the hosts so that the brown was lightened into a winelike amber. Prohibition had turned the city into a landscape of speakeasies and secret parties that weren't very secret; here, the whiskey had come down from Canada and needed to be rationed.

Mostly, the drinking glasses were old jars, and Arch took a less-filthy one and tried to wipe it down with his shirttail.

"The booze will sterilize it," Russ shouted over the noise. "Don't be such a ninny."

Russ had effectively just ended their friendship, but Arch said nothing. His attentions were elsewhere now, in this instance an attractive girl staring frankly at him from her place in the corner with her girlfriends. All the girls in the room were attractive, being culled for their work by the casting offices of Manhattan, but there was something slyly striking about this one.

Drink in hand, he walked straight to her.

"Aren't you the bold one," she said when he got to her. She was having to nearly shout over the noise.

"Show people are that way," he shouted. "Especially low-class show people."

"Is that what you are?"

"Look around. I thought that's what we all are."

She smiled.

"Well, you are in a show, aren't you?"

"No," she said. "I take tickets. I came with these girls. They're in the show. You want to meet them?"

"Not especially."

"I like that, actually."

"Tell me about yourself," he shouted.

"Here? Really?"

"Anyplace you'd like."

She led him out of the apartment and they sat themselves on the low granite blocks that fronted the building. She had cigarettes so they smoked, and she said, "What were you asking me?"

"Where you came from."

"The West Village."

"I mean originally."

"Ever heard of Pennsylvania?"

"Of course I have."

"Not that far away, but far enough away. I grew up in Easton."

"What brought you to New York?"

"The opportunity to take tickets at all the best theaters."

"Are you usually a performer, though?"

"I used to think I was a dancer."

"What made you think differently?"

"The auditions."

"But you're here to stay?"

"I can't go back to Easton," she said. "There's nothing there for me."

She took a drink from her jar and said, "Are you from Boston?"

"I was, once. Now I'm here."

"What do you do?"

"Anything I can. I'm just finishing a short run in a show, but I don't know what's next."

"You're an actor?"

"Somewhat. More of an acrobat. But I hope for stage roles."

"I prefer the moving pictures."

"Well, I'm on the stage."

"The pictures will make the stage obsolete."

"Not unless they find a way you can talk in the pictures. People still want to hear voices. It's human nature."

"Well, you do have a pleasant voice."

"They still don't even let me talk on the stage."

"Why, do you want to talk on the stage?"

"Of course I want to talk on the stage!"

"Maybe you're not so good at it. Talking on the stage, I mean."

"My experiences so far make me worry about that."

"Be in the movies. Then you don't have to talk. You just move your mouth, and you smile a lot."

"Yes, we've established that, haven't we?"

She nodded.

"Well, I'm glad that's settled!"

"Would you like to come to my room?" she said.

"Well, I suppose so," he said.

They walked up Sixth Avenue to the West Village, and then down a side street. At a rather large brick building squatting incongruously among the townhouses, she stopped.

"This is it," she said. "Thank you for escorting me."

The small sign in front of the building: *Ladies Christian Union.*

"You live here?"

"Yes."

"But it's a women's residence."

"And I, sir, am a woman."

"And you want me to come up to your room?"

"Of course I do."

"They just let men walk right in?"

"Of course they don't."

"Then what do you propose?"

"I have no idea."

"If you'd just wanted me to escort you home, you might have just said so. I would have, you know."

"I know, because you're a gentleman."

"Well, shall I come up?"

"I'd like you to."

"How do you propose we accomplish this?"

She pointed up at the third-floor row of windows.

"I'm right up there," she said. "If you can find your way in, I'd be happy to entertain you."

"Explain that one!"

"Wait five minutes and you'll see a window open. And if you can get through that window without being found out, I'd be happy for your company."

"That's a clever trick. You think I can fly through a third-floor window?"

"You said you're an acrobat."

"Well, touché to that!"

"Well, watch for the window. The least I can do is blow you a kiss."

"At this point, I'll take that."

She smiled and climbed the steps and went through the front door. He stood on the sidewalk with his hands in his pockets and watched the windows, shadowed from the streetlight by the sidewalk trees.

Then a window at the far right of the row rumbled open. She eased her head out the window. She said in a hoarse whisper, "You never told me your name."

"Archie. So I'll see you around, then."

"No, really, come on up," she whispered, smiling, and with that withdrew her head into the darkness.

Arch stood for a while waiting for the window to close, but it did not. He looked around and began to imagine how one could find his way to said portal. Impossible would be the first instinct, unless she let her hair down. But he now looked at the challenge as the skilled professional, trained by Bob Pender. And he began to piece it together.

Next door, there was a three-story town house with a roofline not far from the open window. Its brick façade was nearly blank, and so without foothold. But he walked down the street and found that there was, next, a town house with a series of faux wrought-iron balconies and prominent lintels set like shelves at the window tops. This, then, would be his first challenge.

He crouched deeply and then exploded into a leap. In the air, then. At full extension, he stretched even more, and just got his hands on the iron bars, swinging so that he banged his knees hard against the bricks. But he seemed not to be hurt. Onward, then.

Climbing from balcony to balcony was not effortless; each succeeding handhold was nearly out of reach. But he was afire with the urge to get through that window. Making it to the rain gutter at the top was the truest gamble. He would need to jump slightly downward to get his hands on it, with no idea if the gutter was attached solidly enough to bear his weight. He'd only find out when he got there. But he was feeling no fear at all now.

He jumped again, seizing the gutter on his way by. And despite a hefty cracking sound, it somehow held. He pulled himself up onto the roof now, and then stepped along the roof of the next building until that open window was only three feet away.

He spread himself like an X to dangle over and get his hand on her windowsill. He knew this was the payoff moment. He could have asked himself then if he really wanted her that badly; he realized that what he wanted now, more than anything else, was to succeed at the trick. Thirty feet below him was pavement, and that girded him. And with a deep breath and a mighty push of his foot, he was hanging on to her windowsill, pulling himself through the opening, spent.

"*Shhhh,*" she intoned. He got up on his knees. He couldn't see anything in the dark. But there was a small candle lighted; his eyes adjusted. There she was, on the bed, naked.

Afterward, she cried, at some length. Low and huffing sobs. He lay next to her, quiet, with no idea what he could say to console her.

When her tears began to abate, she said, "I'm sorry . . ."

"No, I'm sorry," he said. "I haven't really done this before . . ."

"You haven't ever climbed through a third-floor window?"

"That, either."

She turned and looked at him. "Really? Your first time?"

"More or less."

"How old are you?"

"Twenty. How old are you?"

"Twenty-eight."

"Oh. I didn't realize."

"Why? Did that spoil it for you?"

"Not at all. But I can't help but imagine I'm not your first."

"Sorry to disappoint. Is this how you think a Christian lady loses her virginity?"

"No, not at all."

"You want an explanation for my reaction, then."

"No, it all seems clear. But perhaps some . . . critiquing?"

"Oh! No, no! It wasn't that at all. You were just fine for a beginner."

"Faint praise, indeed."

She took a breath and said, "There was a reason I chose you."

"You chose me?"

"As soon as you walked in the room."

"That happens."

"Yes, you're a very pretty boy. And in truth, you reminded me of a very pretty boy I used to know. A long time ago."

"So why don't you go sleep with him?"

"That's not nice."

"I'm sorry. I take it back."

"Are you cross with me?"

"I suppose not. Just feel second-best. I do wonder why you're not with him, though."

"That's no longer possible, if you see what I mean."

"I'm just the understudy, then."

"Did you even like me, or was it just the challenge of getting what you wanted?"

He was quiet to that, and said, "Did this boy disappoint you?"

"In a way. He turned my life in a different direction. This was before the war. He was going away, to fight. And I became, well . . . as they say, *pregnant*."

"You have a child?"

"I had a child. The baby went away, too. I had to give it up."

"Why?"

"The plan had been that when he came back we'd get married. I was sent away, so no one would know about my condition. But then he was killed. Three weeks after he got there. Somewhere in Belgium. And so the baby went, too. And I couldn't go home. The shame and all. That's why I'm here."

Arch sat up in the bed.

"So you just abandoned your own child? Why, that's a terrible thing to do!"

She looked, in the weak light, as if he had just struck her.

"Don't be cruel to me. You'd only understand if you were in the situation."

He thought better of what he wanted to say.

"And I reminded you of that boy."

"I didn't think you'd mind so much," she said.

"I suppose I didn't, not so very much."

She had gone blank now in the dark, staring at the ceiling. He snapped on the lamp next to the bed and said, "I should go."

She said nothing.

He stood to get dressed. On the night table was a movie magazine, open to a photo page. In one photo, Fairbanks and Pickford were at a beach with friends, all with their arms raised in what the caption said was the fascist salute, which they learned from their friend Mussolini.

"I met them once," he said. "Fairbanks and Pickford."

"I'm sure you did."

"On a ship. Just for a brief moment."

"Still, though. I'm envious."

"So you really do like the movies."

"I adore the movies. Maybe you can take me some time."

"I will, if you like."

"Come back here at three today, and meet me on the front steps."

"Yes. But I don't know your name."

"Celia," she said.

He was dressed now, and went to the door to let himself out.

"No," she said. "You mustn't. They'll see you."

"It's almost dawn. No one will see me."

"The woman at the front desk will see you."

"She won't know I'm coming from this specific room, will she?"

"If they catch me, they'll make me leave. I can't afford anyplace else."

"Then how do I get out?"

"The same way you came in, obviously."

He shook his head and said, "Well, I think not." She was staring him down. He went to the window and sat on the sill. The sidewalk was three stories down.

He could barely remember how he'd gotten in. With the predawn light in the sky, he clambered out. Gone now was the fueled determination he'd had on the way up. He was feeling scared, and tried to put it out of his mind. The leap back to the townhouse's rain gutter would be the crucial move, and he knew it would be harder, as he was trying to launch upward. He breathed in and out, then realized he'd been doing this for a long time. He was frightened, but he had to make his move. The ache of his knees felt keener. There was no line of retreat now.

A pause, a deep breath, and the leap. He was untethered now, hung in a dark sky. Then he caught the gutter like a trapeze. A fraction of a second had passed but it had felt like half his life. He hung there on the creaking gutter until he regathered his strength, maybe a few more seconds but like another half-life, wondering if the handhold would break free before he had the strength to pull himself up.

And then he was on the roof. Everything from here was easy. He realized he was shaking.

The rain was coming down lightly when he got to her building, but Celia was outside quickly with an umbrella. She opened it and pulled him underneath with her and said, "What shall we see?"

"Let's check what's at the Capitol."

The walk was mostly quiet. She asked him who his favorite stars were and he named them as a list. Fairbanks, Tom Mix, Barrymore.

"All the leading men," she said. "Don't you like any women?"

"Certainly, I like women! Lillian Gish rather does it, doesn't she?"

Celia said she adored Valentino, of course. Then there was Pickford and Swanson and Marion Davies. She related stories she'd read in her movie magazines.

"Valentino and Davies made the most money last year," she said. "Valentino made seventy-five hundred a week. How much do you make a week?"

"About thirteen fifty," he said. "But now the show is closing."

"Well, I get paid fourteen, so there. Can you imagine seventy-five hundred? In a week?"

"I can't. But I'd very much like to."

"Is money important to you?"

"As important as it is to anybody, I suppose."

"Is there anything that's especially important to you, more than to anybody else?"

He thought about that as they walked.

"Feeling as if there's someplace I really belong, I suppose."

"That's refreshingly honest. Don't you feel you do now?"

"I'm always on my way someplace else."

The rain was beginning to pick up so she pressed in closer to him, but he didn't think it meant anything. He knew that at the end of the movie they'd part, last names unknown to each other, unlikely to cross paths again in a very large city.

And in the darkness of the theater, up in the balcony with its fifteen-cent tickets, they settled in. The first picture was *The Luck o' the Foolish*, starring Harry Langdon and Marcelline Day. He liked the Mack Sennett comedies but hadn't really truly noticed Langdon, until now. Harry, the doe-eyed innocent, traveling by train with his new bride, and within the close confines of the Pullman car, finding himself in all manner of problem. The first roar that came up in the theater was an acclamation of the actor's subtle art. Langdon wasn't doing the broad and death-defying Harold Lloyd tricks, nor was he Chaplin's clownish Tramp. He was the kind of man people didn't notice as he stumbled through his life. Only the camera saw him, and now the audience as well. Langdon's gestures were nearly invisible but the audience roared again. Archie knew he was watching a genius. A scene in which Langdon was shaving in the jostling train's lavatory but was accidentally nicking another man's neck—only obvious by the man's reaction—was totally believable. The laughter in the theater was unabated now. The girl, laughing as well, slapped his arm, and hard. He realized he'd almost forgotten she was even there.

1959

HIS SESSIONS HAVE MADE him understand things so differently. Inner revelation has again left him feeling entrapped in his rather well-wrought self.

It bears recollection, the Acrobat thinks, that even young Arch had been filled with a desperation of his own. He wasn't above using deceit to move himself forward, though at the time he had congratulated himself on having taken a far more elegant solution, that of the entertainer's art. The codified and socially acceptable lies of the stage were a transference that could have gone elsewhere. Could he see himself as having become a confidence man or, God forbid, a politician? Regrettably, yes. Pressing trousers all day would never have cut it.

But has he gotten away that easy? A lie is a lie, after all, and he's piled them up, ever since. He wasn't actually Roger Thornhill, or John Robie, or Nickie Ferrante; as the years have gone by, he's not even sure he's Archie anymore. But lying, be it crude or be it artful, had become his nature and his tradecraft.

To wit: today's sudden inspiration. Sometimes this carefully curated persona feels just a bit tight-fitting. It's good to be the king, most of the time. But not all of the time.

He phones the best makeup artist he knows.

"Bob, my friend, how would you like a new challenge?"

"Why not? What should I bring?"

"Well, bring everything," the Acrobat says. "I'll send my car."

Bob Schiffer, an old hand at the studio and highly regarded for his cosmetic illusions, arrives lugging a silver aluminum suitcase weighted with its paraphernalia, and he's smiling at the oddness of this all.

"The man who invented Rita Hayworth," the Acrobat says.

"That was actually your friend Howard Hughes," Bob says. "But I helped a little with the look, I suppose."

Bob has been around a long time, his own story not far different than the Acrobat's. He shipped out at fifteen on an ocean liner, lying about his age to become an apprentice seaman. He began his truer career making up female passengers for shipboard balls. Someone noticed. He was at MGM by the time he was sixteen. He's fortyish now, a man at the top of his game.

"I have a challenge for you, Bob. I want you to erase me. Make me someone people don't even notice as he walks by."

"What picture is all this for?" Bob says.

"Not a specific one, yet. Think of this as an artist's study. But it has to look good in the world. It needs to look real up close."

Bob seems intrigued but asks no details.

"Yeah, I can do that. What I can probably do is make you look like a man who sort of looks like you, but isn't you. A man who's missing your essence. An 'almost-but-not-really' kind of guy."

"Oh, I'd love that!"

They sit facing each other on dining-room chairs, the makeup kit open on the table. Bob begins by carefully filling in the chin cleft with a thin putty, the first step to muting the Acrobat's essence. What an odd sensation—no one has ever denied him that.

Bob sits back at that, considering.

"Just that makes a huge difference," he says. "My God, I feel like I've stolen a bit of your soul."

"You know, in my early days on contract the studio airbrushed my chin. They said it was suggestive."

"Suggestive of what?"

"If you must know, they likened my chin to genitalia. But when they stopped doing it, my career began to take off."

"The studio is prone to airbrushing away one's character," Bob says. Then, "No hints for me at all on what this is for?"

"None at all, Bob. Let's see what you can do. Make it enough to pass a very tight close-up."

"All right, then, let's give you a bit of a beard."

In his case he has a box of peltlike prosthetic facial hair. The one he selects is gray, a kind of low-slung goatee. Bob applies some rubber cement and flattens it just south of the now-nonexistent chin cleft.

Two hours with the work, the Acrobat never looking toward a mirror. Bob talks mostly about baseball, the Dodgers, Koufax, Duke Snider. Each of them has been in the pictures long enough not to be wanting to talk about the pictures. The work begins on his hair, then proceeds to his skin, then to the smallest contours of his features.

"Let's see your teeth," Bob says.

The Acrobat opens his mouth and retracts his lips to make a grimacing smile. Bob seems to be caught in himself.

"Wait a minute . . ."

"That's right. I have an odd smile in an even-numbered world."

"I'll be damned," Bob says, and then, "So let me tone down all this dazzling whiteness."

He has a brush to which he applies a brackish liquid. "This will discolor them, at least until you give them a good brushing."

Bob is looking at him as if at a canvas, the artist considering his work.

"Want some glasses? They're all nonprescription." He finds a plain-looking pair with a clear-acetate frame.

Finally, Bob steps back and nods at his work.

"That ought to do it," he says.

The Acrobat rises from the chair and walks to the mirror by the buffet. He's stunned.

"Who is this poor fellow?" he says, feeling the tightness of the work as he smiles.

"So? Yes?" Bob says.

"Yes, indeed. Me, but not me at all. Do you think people

could tell, if I went out this way?"

"Nah. They'd think something was a little off about you, but nobody will be looking for makeup."

"Good."

"Want me to take it off now?"

"Oh, no, we're done for now. I'm going to do a little walking around, in someone else's shoes."

"Getting in character? Are you adopting the Method?"

"No, my methods are my own, and have always been. You must be thinking of Brando."

"I try to think of him as little as possible," Bob says as he packs up and takes the cash. "He's going to ruin acting."

1924

ON THE NINTH OF February the snows blew into Manhattan. By that night, ten inches or more had topped off the snow that had fallen heavily a week before. The storm showed no sign of abating. Arch trudged crosstown with his bag in one hand and his stilts over his shoulder, looking for someone to take him in. He'd run out of money and the rooming house was hearing no more about IOUs from a would-be actor. The storm had brought a stream of people looking for refuge, shut out with the hotels suddenly full, and who would pay what it took. Arch, ten days late with his rent and two weeks past his twenty-second birthday, was summarily out. The snow stung his face as he imagined who might help him. In truth, a list did not form quickly. Everybody was in the same fix as he was; it all seemed easy in the summer but he wasn't getting hired now and he needed to do what he had to.

As the city darkened again and snow raged on, Arch found

the building off Seventh Avenue, on Commerce Street. The front door swung heavily. Up the narrow stairs, he stomped the snow off. Down the dimly lit hallway and to the apartment door, from behind which he could hear the tinny whine of the phonograph playing "I've Found a New Baby" and the murmur of voices.

Three knocks, and the voices stopped. The volume on the machine dropped. Silence.

Three more quick raps. No answer.

"It's Archie," he called.

Footsteps, and the door opened a few inches. There was the Australian.

"Archie? We thought it might be the police."

"Police? On what charge?"

"Any bloody one of them!" the Aussie said. "And we'd be guilty!"

"Can I come in?"

The Aussie looked suspicious.

"For what?"

Arch had first come across the Aussie at one of the endless afterparties. Like Arch, he was embroidering his own illusory persona—artist, designer, sage. These were aspirations, not lies: As for the truth of it, he never denied who he was at the core. The Aussie was seven years older than Arch, an age at which one might abandon such larks. He didn't seem exceedingly bright, but he had an undeniable and intuitive charm. At one particular party, Arch found himself enthralled. The magnetic attraction to the energy, and the confidence, as he'd had to Fairbanks for that instant. And as with Fairbanks, he studied the Aussie, looking to pick out of him one true thread he could make into his own.

Now, he stood at the door of this man, aware that in fact they hardly knew each other. The Aussie was in a silk dressing gown, and holding a drink, and was unshaven.

"What do you want?" he said. Another man stood back in the shadows.

"Well, the thing is . . ."

"We only have enough liquor for Charlie and myself," the Aussie said, as if settling the matter.

"It's more complicated than that. I need a place to stay."

"Well, so long as you get your own liquor."

"That's fine."

"And you'll need to sleep on the floor."

"It's the best offer I've had in some time."

"You look absolutely awful, boy."

"I feel awful," Arch said.

"Have you been skiing out there?"

"Oh. No, these are my stilts."

"Tools of the jester's trade."

"Yes, I suppose so."

"And how very sad that is."

The Aussie's name was Jack Kelly, which he hated for its plainness. Jack also had once mocked Archie's name as hopelessly arriviste for a boy from the lower classes. Archibald, my God! Arch had no idea.

"This is Charlie Phelps," Jack said, nodding toward the figure sitting in a chair by the phonograph, deciding which records to play. "But onstage, Charlie goes by the name Spangles."

Charlie nodded at Arch as he entered, but said nothing. Charlie was in a kimono, but with a heavy sweater over it to battle the drafts from the rattling windows.

Arch could see Jack observing Charlie observing Arch observing Jack. And Jack loved it, clearly.

"What in God's name happened in your life that you're showing up at our door?" Jack said, an amused edge to the question.

"I couldn't pay my rent. I don't have any jobs, and I'm not making enough money with the stilt-walking."

"I thought you were an actor."

"I haven't been cast enough yet."

"What have you done? As far as acting?"

"I've been working on a magic act with another fellow. I go by Know-All Leach."

"That's rather tragic, isn't it?"

"As I say, I haven't landed any good roles yet."

"Ah, yes, the eternal 'Yet.'"

"I'll make it."

"I know you're a tumbler, but what does that have to do with being an actor? You're a beautiful boy, to be sure, but lots of beautiful boys are roaming these streets, aren't they?"

"I suppose."

"What's in the bag?"

"A couple of suits, three shirts, six neckties, and underwear."

"All the worldly possessions, then? Your entire act a sad little satchel?"

"It's everything I need," Arch said. "It's a simple life."

Jack pointed at an open spot on the bare floor. "There's your bed, fellow."

Arch knew what Jack was, and what Charlie was as well. No one had ever explained people like that to him, but they were all around in show business and it made no difference to him. And why would he care? People taking him in off the street were inherently good people. Simple as that. His own pangs and infatuations were rather liberal as well. He rang it up to his general enthusiasm for life.

He also could not say this was bliss, as Jack was ambitious

and complicated. Jack had a way about him, both soft and rough, and his professed goal was to be an actor, just like everybody else. Charlie Spangles had even more of a way, and winningly so. Spangles was a pastiche of gender, and performed around the Village as exactly that. One of the bits was as a person divided down the middle: on one side a woman in a dress, on the other a man in a tuxedo. Jack had painstakingly stitched the outfit together. Spangles played both sides convincingly. Jack called Spangles "they," in tribute to the twinned identities. Jack once mumbled the word *Hermaphroditus*, which Arch inferred might mean something but lacked the schooling to know. The word was said with the unmistakable tone that Arch understood, which he did in the larger sense while ignorant of details. Arch was grateful for shelter and whatever friendship that entailed. Spangles had a warmer affect than Jack but also saved most energy for the stage.

The domesticity was jarring, after a silent childhood in a silent home. Arch was not quite the ward, but Jack still took on a patronizing air. Jack had arching eyebrows that curved down to a nose and pursed mouth set in a heavy face; it was a deadpan countenance with a gush of wildness beneath it. One of those people you meet in the business and its endless competitions. Arch was likewise embraced and embedded, part of a cacophony that was like bringing the ruckus of the stage home. Noise as a warm garment, in which he happily wrapped himself.

Life was a looping hustle. Onto the stilts by day, navigating streets with lofty regard and pining for the true boards, to stand on a legitimate stage in the thrall of these same people who brushed by him on the wide (and these days, icy) city sidewalks. The Aussie brought some melodrama to the proceedings, always with a scheme.

By night they made neckties, Arch cutting the dies and Jack

with his tiny paintbrushes, applying his adornments.

"The real money comes when you add your own design," Jack said. "It's all about putting down your own mark. Which I always do. Everywhere."

Jack had a confidence Arch studied, deeply. Jack, in turn, began to assay Arch's raw mettle. Arch, in his rumpled Bristol wardrobe, thinking that a shining face and clever feet would ever get him through.

That little studio at 21 Commerce Street: Arch had a home to go to, rather than to escape from. And as he sought less refuge at the theater, the theater grudgingly found a home for him. Bit parts in vaudeville began to materialize, mostly, as he was now old enough to play a man. His face was annealing into something, less soft than before, an angularity made of one part hormones and two parts starvation. When the cold weather blew through Lower Manhattan and the shows were hothouses of spotlights and cavernous laughter, Arch walked home through the teeth of winds blowing down narrow streets, finally to the unheated apartment. One frigid night, Jack urged him to join him in bed under his heavy comforter, premising the double duty of two generators fueling light and power. Arch climbed in, nearly disoriented by the softness of the bed. Spangles often came thumping in with the first light and closed the blinds to the first shafts of sunshine, keeping night blissfully alive. It was a time of lumpy mattresses set on floors, and the heady smell of Jack's paint cans, and clothing hung over chairs, and scarce food wrapped in pilfered hotel napkins.

Ambition was what it was, but the moment was what it was, too. Arch was bringing in enough money to eat, had a place to stay and some friends. He wondered if that was what made people stop their climb, that satisfaction with the moment they occupied. He felt that, but he knew he was hopelessly hoping for things bigger, shinier, and more rewarding. Almost as suddenly as he thought it, he had the creeping sensation Jack had suddenly deciphered him, and the tension set in with immediacy.

Then illness. Wracked with fevers, making it through shows in a blank sweat and fighting the winds as if they had pierced his skin. Coughing in the night, he opened his eyes to see Jack.

"You need to be seen by a doctor, Archie."

"I don't have the money."

"Then I'll have to pay for it."

The doctor came up that next morning and diagnosed pneumonia. Fluids and rest and hope. Jack handed the doctor a five-dollar bill, the equal of a week's food.

Even after Arch began to feel better, he kept pretending he was sick. In those days, everything seemed like "acting practice," and that became a form of gentle evasion from Jack. And the equation turned once more. Arch was beholden, yet again. As he came out of the illness and things became more normal, the gratitude had begun to weigh heavy. Even Spangles was picking up on the shift in the air, saying one night when Arch and Jack sat not speaking to each other, "Why is no one being amusing?"

But he needed money and it was Jack who got him into an unexpected gig.

He began to socialize in service of a clientele of middle-aged women for whom he acted as a paid escort. Jack had put him on to this, intimating it was a way of paying past debts, and assuring him it was on the level. The task, of course, necessitated formal attire, with the destination typically being the theater. He was hired to look good, be quick with a cigarette lighter, and remain judicious with any chatter. He was well aware he was serving as background. He served as a seat filler at formal dinners, to ensure the boy-girl-boy-girl arrangement. At those dinners, he mostly listened. At least at first. This was his higher education. To hear these people was to glean not only their knowledge but also their preoccupations, their manners, their tribal rites, their fears and their perceptions. When he began to return volley, he surprised people. They looked at him wondering where he fell on the Social Register. Acting practice, he reckoned. Speaking to them in the Fairbanks voice, which he'd made his own. To find Archie Leach in the Waldorf-Astoria, involved in a discussion of the migratory patterns of Humboldt penguins, might have been surprising to Elias Leach, or Bob Pender for that matter. When Arch was the one who was holding forth on the penguins, even more so. He'd picked it all up at a previous dinner, thought it a lark to repeat it, and found that people bought his act.

"And when did you last find yourself in Chile?" a woman across the table asked.

"Oh, not in some time," he said, in a jocular diversion. "Not in quite some time!"

Jack, meanwhile, started getting work in West Village speakeasies, painting murals. The jobs suited him: his love of secrecy and scandal, of being an insider, of illicit pleasure. And his being away more from the apartment was a relief. Arch was someone used to decamping; he felt an escape drawing nigh. He was saving his dollars until he could pay back the doctor's fee, and offer some sort of retroactive rent, and get out of the apartment in which he knew he was an interloper.

One night, at another formal dinner with another forgettable woman, Arch sat across the table from a man who couldn't stop looking at him. Not that he wasn't used to it. But this was different, more businesslike, a mien of calculation instead of ardor.

"Say there, are you Australian?" the man said. "I can't place that accent."

"Actually, I'm not."

"Well, would you like to be Australian?"

The man introduced himself as Reggie Hammerstein. Brother of Oscar, of whom Arch had most definitely heard. But Reggie, a theatrical producer, had a show coming up, and he had a small part for Arch if he could be an Aussie.

"Sure as hell!" he said in Jack's best voice, and a few people smiled, at this young uptown gent mimicking some working-class lout. Not a long stretch for the accent, really, because he had already been absorbing Jack's: Some of the West Village boys had begun calling him "Kangaroo" based on their assumption of who he was, and where he was from. All wrong, as usual.

That quickly, Arch was suddenly no longer the ward, no longer the charity case, no longer the second banana. Arch could see Jack's slow burn as Arch began to attract the attention of showgirls, ingenues, and singers, all blond and all as ambitious as he was. The show, *Golden Dawn*, paid seventy-five dollars a week. As rehearsals began in the afternoons, he got himself by at night, escorting more ladies until the first paycheck came. Gone early in the day, and back very late.

"Yet he always comes home to me" was Jack's nightly punch line.

"Calm yourself," Arch shot back one night as Jack surveyed him from the bed, in his dressing gown. "It's not manly."

"You mean, manly like you?" Jack said, rising with clenched fists.

Arch clenched his fists right back, and after they'd both stood snorting for a bit, the moment passed. Jack said, "Knew you were afraid, you pathetic slag," and lay back down. Then he said, "Why don't you listen to anything I say? I'm telling you that the only way to move forward is to keep being who you're becoming."

"I agree completely," Arch said, speaking as someone who would be anything he needed to be in any given moment.

Jack sat up in bed.

"I assume you'll be vacating the premises."

"Of course."

"Well, I'll offer a parting thought for you."

"Unload at will."

"You have no class, boy."

"That's it? You need to muster a better attack than that, Jack."

"No, I mean it quite seriously. It's time. If there's one thing all these shows and movies try to give people, it's the idea that class matters. That's the sign of a person who matters. I don't mean education or breeding or refinement, either. I mean something you still need to find. You're a product of the lower classes."

"My father is a tailor's presser," Arch said. "Why, what's yours?"

"A *tailor*," Jack said, with a finality in his tone.

"I also left school early, but that was my own choice."

"Then you need to compensate."

"How?"

"You've been pretending to be better, but you treat it as a joke. Maybe don't."

"How can it not be a joke?"

"You need to act as if you have something people want," Jack said, and for once sincerely. "Whatever that may be. Looks can't carry the day. There has to be more. I can tell you about how to wear clothes, and how to have manners. But you need to believe the charade completely if anyone else is going to believe it."

He found his way to Forty-Second Street and the public library, where he was able to unshelve Emily Post's *Etiquette in Society, in Business, in Politics, and at Home,* and study it as if a Sanskrit manuscript, amazed and enthralled by all the arcane rules he'd never known. And in those small admonitions seemed rules of life as important as the Ten Commandments. *The joy of joys is the person of light but unmalicious humor. If you know anyone who is gay, beguiling and amusing, you will, if you are wise, do everything you can to make him prefer your house and your table to any other; for where he is, the successful party is also. What he says is of no matter, it is the twist he gives to it, the intonation, the personality he puts into his quip or retort or observation that delights his hearers, and in his case the ordinary rules do not apply.*

One late afternoon, his head full of the nuances of place settings (and confounded by the very fact of meat forks and fish forks), Arch was passing the Hotel Astor. A late-winter dusk settled outside. Lights had just begun to flicker in windows and storefronts. Hands in his pockets, head down, he was shuffling along Broadway. And then ahead, a woman. The svelte walk; even by her backside he somehow knew who it was. He'd been to all the movies; that swaybacked gait. He's just recently seen *The Temptress*, and that woman was undoubtedly she. Garbo herself.

He was amazed she was alone. A silk scarf was half covering her face. People just walked past her, clinching their own collars against the cold, somehow unaware. That was the funny thing, when someone so big could not be imagined on a common sidewalk. On she went and he fell in a distance behind her, following but without plan or prospect.

It didn't occur to him he was doing anything wrong. Starstruck and curious in equal measure, he wanted to see where she'd go, whom she was to meet, or what she did when she wasn't on the big screen. She moved onward, in no hurry, apparently without worry on the streets of the city. Headed north, she seemed uninterested in the taxicabs and trolleys and occasional hansoms that streamed along on the street.

He thought she might be headed toward Central Park. Or maybe meeting a man, he thought with a curious pang of dejection. He'd read the tabloids and knew she was linked to John Gilbert, "The Great Lover," as he was called; they'd just starred together in *Flesh and the Devil.* He heartened, that Gilbert might be ahead, and the terminus of a stealthy assignation.

But at Fifty-Ninth Street, instead of crossing to the edge of the park, she turned right and he realized her destination was the Plaza. At the hotel, she didn't remove her scarf as she entered. At the front desk, she took her room key from the inscrutable deskman and then moved on to the elevator, where the operator puffed his chest as if a palace guard, and Archie shrank back from the man's glare.

He left the lobby and stepped back onto the street. That was the difference between being a star and not: that you were recognized and followed even when you didn't realize it. For stars, there were eyes on you even when you couldn't see them. He looked around, and as yet saw no one.

Casting calls. Auditions. Trying to get a foot in the door, being judged and trying to glean the small approvals and disapprovals that would shape his success. Of course, they'd never say it right out. He had to watch for the small signs, hear the silences and sense the mood. Thus far, his instincts had utterly failed him.

Today he was reading for a small part in a production in which the chosen actor would play a youthful scion. He sat in a waiting room full of young men in their twenties, and he could only speculate about where they came from. But this was New York City, in the ongoing postwar boom, and many a boy had come to the city seeking an easy life they were realizing wasn't so easy at all. *Golden Dawn* had closed, and he was back in the hunt.

Auditions were like courting, prone to overwrought hopes,

deep embarrassment, and subsequent despair; trying to guess why one had turned out not to be good enough was an exercise in self-flagellation. But the need to produce a product that buyers wanted was a simple transaction. Archie watched the others carefully, trying to guess what success looked like.

The boy next to him on the long bench looked close to retching. He was natty and pale, clothed in a red-and-navy striped blazer and bow tie that suggested he might soon be off for a round of croquet. The role they were all reading for was innocuous, the rather louche younger brother of the main character. They'd been told little else. The boy in the striped jacket appeared whiter than normal, through Arch had never seen him before.

"Are you all right?" Arch finally said. The boy turned to him with a nearly pleading look. "You look a bit ill."

"Is it really that apparent?" the boy said, straightening up.

"I may have been mistaken. Disregard that."

"But I can't now just disregard it, can I?"

"Well, try breathing more."

"I feel I'm already breathing quite too much."

"Then disregard that as well."

The boy turned and gave him a more considered look.

"What's your game, friend?"

"Really none. None at all. In fact, disregard me completely."

"I'll certainly try!"

The boy crossed his arms over his chest and stared ahead, but Arch could still hear his labored breathing.

The auditions were inside the theater, through double swinging doors that flapped with each ingress and egress of another hopeful actor. One by one, the other boys were called, by a secretary with her clipboard. As the room dwindled, the awkwardness between Arch and the boy next to him was getting heavier. He thought about moving to another spot on the benches but feared that too much might be read into that. But then the secretary came out and called, "Dinwiddie!" The boy sprang up.

There were now six of them left of the original thirty or so. After a while, the double doors swung and out came Dinwiddie, even more pale than before. He glared for a moment at Arch and then staggered out toward the street as if a drunk.

Each boy went in and came out. Arch found himself the last on the bench. He tried to imagine his reputation had preceded him, but it was more obvious this was pure chance. But then the secretary, a woman who was tired-looking enough to suggest a long career in the theater world, came out, looked at him, and said, "Are you Leach?"

He sprang to his feet. "Indeed I am."

"Well then you're not needed."

"I beg your pardon?"

"You're not needed."

"How is that?"

"Well, your name's been crossed off."

"Why?"

"That's not your affair."

"But I've been here four hours."

"And we appreciate your patience."

"I'm confused. Does it mean I'll be sent straight to a callback?"

"No, it certainly doesn't mean that at all."

"Then I most assuredly don't understand."

"Let us say," she said, "that we decided we don't need your type."

Months later, he went to the theater and slipped into the play during intermission, walking back in with the smokers and following the stream of people climbing the stairs up to the balcony. He stood in the back and waited for the character of the louche younger brother to appear. He had begun to convince himself Dinwiddie would be in that role, but the actor who came on was someone he didn't remember from the auditions. He felt relieved. He saw a boy a bit more stocky than himself, with blond hair that nearly mirrored the light. Maybe that was the difference. The actress playing the older sister was a blonde; it made some sense this actor had been chosen. The louche brother's lines were mostly quips, and mostly not funny. Arch left the theater and walked back to the rooming house he was now calling home.

But he found himself keeping an eye out for Dinwiddie. He was burning to know why he hadn't been called that day. He asked around and no one had heard the name. A girl he knew worked in an agent's offices, where they kept an actor's directory one could pay to be entered into. But the name did not come up (his was not there, either; too much money). In time, he gave it up. He imagined that as the boy's only try at the theater world, a onetime rejection that probably sent him packing, embarrassed, back to the family homestead, wherever that might have been. Most people didn't have the stomach for the theater. Even when you had a job, when that job ended you were back in purgatory. It required a fortitude of an unexpected kind.

A Hall of **D**oors

HE LEAVES HIS DRESSING *room and walks across the darkened expanse of the soundstage, ready to go home. He's shot more of the predictable scenes of another predictable picture, the easy success of doing what you do well. The gaffers have shut down all the main lights so that he follows a dim trail of illumination toward the red of the stage-door light.*

He opens the door and goes through. But he's now on another soundstage. The sheer size of the movie business's great spaces so daunting, so able to create any world inside its walls, to replicate vast cities and lost civilizations. Far across the way, the red light of this stage's exit door. He rather enjoys the solitude of the building sometimes. He hadn't intended a stroll, but he feels relaxed and in no hurry.

A movie set is made of two sides. On one side, it is a dazzle of brightly lit illusions, glistening and convincingly real to the eye.

Actors live their lives in this half shell, the day side of a hemispherical planet. Then, across a line is the darkness behind the lights, and the jumble of the machinery that fuels the illusion, and the people unseen in the world of the picture, who exist within inches of the image but will never be in the image. And then all the lights go out and the world ceases to exist.

He opens the next door and is now in a dark hallway. At the end of it is the exit door. He'll need to get his bearings once outside, and to find his car. But the studio is familiar terrain and he'll get where he needs to.

But through that door, he finds not a parking lot but another empty soundstage. Now he's confused. Where has he made his wrong turn?

He turns around and goes back through the door, but he's not back in the hallway, but on another darkened stage. It seems as if he's miscalculated, or misremembered.

"Hello?" he calls. "Is anyone here?" The echoes peal back at him from the black vastness. But no one calls back.

But there's another door he didn't see and he walks to it and opens it, to find another darkened stage. The darkness seems even deeper. He has no sense of how far the walls are from him, or how high the rafters. He has no idea which direction to take.

"Can someone please help me?" he calls into the darkness.

1931

OLD LONG HIGHWAYS, SOME no more than oil sprayed over gravel; some roads just swaths of ravined mud, others just hard-rutted prairie. But they were heading west. New York was done now, Hollywood the shining prize. Arch behind the Saturn's ring of a steering wheel of his Packard Phaeton convertible, bought dear with his windfall of earnings from the last Broadway show. There had been a time when he would have done anything to be on a stage, just for the humid intimacy of a packed house, regardless of the pay. But in *Street Singer*, the traveling Shubert production that had toured around the country for nine months, he'd made four hundred fifty a week, at a time when a working man like his father would have sweated through fifty hours to bring home thirty dollars. And it seemed as if half the country was out of work altogether.

Arch was twenty-seven years old. The Depression had dug in for the long haul. But Arch, who had been poor in the good times, was now rich in the bad times. He was heading west, kissed by the sun. The back of his car was packed with the many fine suits, all bought with his theater earnings and with the certainty the money would continue coming. In the passenger seat was Phil Charig, a composer. Arch and Phil had been planning a late-autumn golf trip to Florida, but their ambitions rather impulsively sent them on a longitudinal course instead. They wanted Hollywood, wanted to think Hollywood needed them, and had put New York away.

They drove south for two days to escape the cold, then pivoted westward. They pulled back the car's convertible top and folded down the windshield; the cold air in their faces was bracing. But they would be suntanned (and wind-burned, and bug-bitten) upon their arrival. Back in New York, the Aussie had likewise been making endless noise about heading to Hollywood. But he'd already found a ride.

The road was long but Arch and Phil rode in style, roaring past lesser fortunes. Looking straight ahead, he could endlessly follow the hood ornament, the Packard's chrome-plated reclining Adonis, sitting pretty on the radiator cap and hitching this ride all the way across the country. In the periphery, the dark and bended forms, off in the distance. The field workers, the pickers dotted all across the vast landscape, making his own presumed struggle seem even more clownish and undeserved. Backs hunched over fields in late-autumn sunlight, ragged, like minor updatings of the peasants of Breughel the Elder, leaning in their wheat stalks. Tobacco and cotton giving way westward to sorghum and wheat, hard crops by hand. Dirt under the fingernails and in the seams of the skin, unwashable in its permanence.

And in every town, they saw the unemployed, sitting on benches or lined up for charity food as if waiting for their stark realities to blessedly lighten. They eyed the Packard not with resentment but with frank admiration. It was a curious reality; somehow they seemed to take pleasure in seeing such a beautiful car among their filthy pickups and shambled Model Ts.

And: a movie house in every backwater town they passed as well. Sometimes, as he and Phil lodged for the night, he'd look out the hotel-room window near dusk and see lines of people in front of the marquee, waiting to file in and hand over their hard-won quarters for two hours of blessed respite and some sustenance of spirit. *The Sidewalks of New York*, *Palmy Days*, *Monkey Business*. The pictures let them laugh and forget.

He'd sat with his friend Fay Wray the night before his departure, nervous. Fay had already done a dozen pictures, and made the jump from silents to talkies. She was a seasoned professional at twenty-four, and he was feeling less so in her presence. They'd met with her mired in a brutal marriage with a drunken, older writer. They were cast in a play called *Nikki*, written by the husband and based on his own short stories. Arch, cast as a soldier named Cary Lockwood who falls in love with her, instantly fell in love with her. And she knew it, even as she demurred. The husband knew it, too, as he watched rehearsals from the seats.

Fay was on the rise but still waiting for something to really grab her and carry her to fame.

"You're a quiet boy, but on the stage you need to play boys who aren't so quiet," she said. "Let the roles tell you who to be. Don't be a quiet man. I doubt that will get you where you want to go."

Hung in the air once again, between lives. He'd turned down a new Shubert show planned for Broadway; his only real brush with the movie studios was that one failed screen test shot ("Your neck is too thick . . .") and a part in a one-reeler called *Singapore Sue*, shot not in Hollywood but in Paramount's soundstage in Astoria, Queens. There was no indication the film was even going to be released. So here he went, westward, ready to redouble. Funny how the Pender Troupe and then the New York stage seemed to have grown small under his feet. People had begun to recognize him, at least in the theater district. Now, in small towns in a vast country, it was the car people noticed, not the men inside; they were being admired by association. Arch planned to change that.

The continental crossing was reminiscent of the Pender Troupe's transatlantic journey; a kind of bridging of worlds. His travels around the Midwest with *Street Singer* were not so much a Broadway tryout as his leading-man tryout. He was established as a journeyman, a veteran, a mercenary. He could feel at home on any stage he walked upon, as long as it started in the brilliant rising glow of Kliegl Brothers footlights, then concluded by going to black and the tailwind of applause; he could then escape into excitable urges. Could he explain the pleasure, then, of dressing himself in the dawn half light in the room of a local he'd met after another night's show? He, the dashing out-of-towner with no strings to attach; a night's partner, finding a little rebellion in a parochial heart. He'd walk back to his hotel in the predawn cold, weightless and sated. He was filled with odd love.

Women, of course, were so fine. He loved them but didn't understand them. Men he understood; he found some of them not so fine, in many instances. To rise from sheets exhaling perfume, to touch that warm skin by sliding his hand under the blanket's clutch, to feel not as alone as those childhood nights with his father gone to the pub and his mother gone for good.

So he'd certainly traveled this country before, in circuitous dance steps, paying half attention as he ran his lines in a train car or caught naps as the landscape slid by. This, now, here, was a different thing: an arrow's straight shot from the gathering cold of Broadway to the shining target under the California sun. One revelation of America was how well he tanned. Back in the pall of Bristol, he'd have never known he had it in him.

What a comfort uncertainty had become in his life! It was when he was settled into something—contracted, cast, and wardrobed—that he felt the rising anxiety. Anything that required him to know where he'd be meant he wasn't free to imagine being someplace better. It was now, driving, letting the Phaeton's hundred and six horses get to full gallop on straight-shot roads, when he felt the soaring possibilities, always onward and always upward.

It had been time for change, anyway. At the end of the autumn traveling run of *Street Singer*, the Shuberts were in financial trouble. They asked Arch to cut his salary by a third, and Arch agreed, then immediately regretted doing so. The blow was softened by their reassurance that he'd be star-billed on the next production; this allowed them to bypass whatever guilt they might have felt, but it also gave Arch an exit without looking as if he were high-hatting them. It didn't mean they weren't shocked, it was just that they couldn't raise righteous arguments after reneging on their contract. But New York already felt old, as old as Bristol had when he'd boarded that ship with the Penders.

He was done with cold and fog and rain. Across Virginia and then Tennessee, the roads turned to dirt as they sailed past fields where laborers stood from their work to witness their passing in the fine car, a signal event in otherwise bleak days. Across the Mississippi at Memphis, the vistas spread out farther. They sometimes saw no one until they pulled into a town to find beds. In Amarillo they stayed in the Santa Fe Hotel and watched the businessmen in the bar with their tailored suits and spotless white cowboy hats, their tooled boots shining glassy. In Arizona, the sun seemed to change. Brighter, somehow, whiter, cleaner. Bigger. The burgundy paint on the Phaeton, which had presented blood-dark as it sat in front of the Belvedere Hotel on West Forty-Eighth Street as he emptied his room and packed the car, but now glowed like ruby against the monochrome desert.

In the Arizona desert they knifed through dry air on cold mornings that turned to high heat and back to the chill of sunset. Through the mountains, the car thrumming upward, and on the tenth day the descent into Los Angeles was nearly overwhelming and then they were pulling in front of the Château Élysée, putting down cash for an extended stay. He'd made a vast middle passage between the city of the stage and the city of the screen. He'd seen three thousand miles of faces needing someone like him to ease them from their troubles.

1959

THE MAKEUP IS AGAIN close to impeccable. Not just enough to fool a camera, but enough to fool the human eye at close range.

And so little used: the chin's telltale cleft duly packed again with putty and powdered over, as his entire face is covered with a light sheen to mute the tan and add a pallid grayness. That first time, he'd left Bob and taken a walk down Sunset Boulevard, unnoticed by passersby. He found he needed more. The hair is sprayed gray and tousled in a way the Acrobat would never be seen in, which is the point. He's let his whiskers grow for three days, and Bob Schiffer has again applied a wisp of beard. All to create the slightest deflections by which he can act out the rest.

The venue is a dusty diner on the edges of Bakersfield, along a commercial strip. He's pulled into the gravel parking lot in a ten-year-old Chevrolet that had been sourced from Props via some stealthy phone calls from a studio assistant. The license in his wallet is the only evidence of his charade. The wallet is thick with one-dollar bills, but nothing larger.

He sits at the counter, head down. The tired workingman, neither poor nor rich, neither sad nor happy, but rather the kind of person who moves through the world nearly invisibly, as normal as everybody else. The waitress, a tired working woman of deep middle age, and equally unremarkable, asks what he'll have.

"Coffee," he says.

She holds her look on him just a bit too long, then walks away. Back with the coffee, she says, "Eats?"

"Not yet."

"So let me know," she says, walking off.

This place is otherworldly in its normality. As real as a 360-degree movie set depicting a diner on a dusty highway, filled with extras feigning the cycles of everyday life. In a corner booth, a young couple whisper furtively, possibly in an argument. A truck driver at a table shoves his hamburger in his mouth, hurrying through his respite from the wheel. And the Acrobat, just another extra in a story with no leads, seeing how the other half lives. To be a person no one takes note of is to reverse every urge he once had.

"This taken?"

He glances up and there's a woman, pointing at the adjacent stool, despite the line of empty ones farther down the counter.

"Suit yourself," he says, mindful of flattening his accent to an American grunt.

She's younger, maybe fortyish, cheaply dressed but neatly so. Bright lipstick, and the light veil of perfume. She seats herself and says, "I work at the jewelry store right down the way."

He suppresses the words that come to his head. *Fancy that!* Too out of character.

"That so?" he says instead. In his head, he hears the words in Jimmy Stewart's voice.

"It is so. How about you?"

"What about me?"

The woman smiles broadly and presses on.

"So what do you do? Where are you from?"

"Just passing through."

"Headed where?"

". . . Tucson."

"Did you have to think about that?"

"Not at all."

"What do you need to do in Tucson?"

"Seeing friends."

"Really? You don't really seem the friendly type."

He takes a long draw of breath and waves to the waitress, who comes over.

"Apple pie."

The waitress nods and then turns to the woman on the stool.

"Nancy, give the man some air, will you?"

"Just getting acquainted," Nancy says. "Just being courteous."

The Acrobat can see that the other people are now aware of him, glancing over to see what's going on. Nancy swivels toward the counter and says to the waitress, "Like always."

She then leans in and whispers, "You on the Most Wanted list or something?"

"Not a chance."

"So I was asking what you do . . ."

The waitress is back quickly, sliding the heavy plate to him, the pie snowcapped with a scoop of vanilla he didn't ask for. He pushes the ice cream off the top with his fork and sees that Nancy is watching him. He swivels at her, squaring up with his hands on his knees and looks hard at her. She shrinks a little, and the eyes drop.

"Nothing that exciting, is what I do."

"What's your name, fella?"

He pauses.

"My name is Charnley," he says.

"Did you have to think about that, too?"

He puts his fork down and gives her a glare.

"Easy does it, mister," Nancy says. "Look, I didn't mean to irritate you."

"Who the hell's irritated?"

"Maybe it's just your manner. Kind of rough-cut."

He shrugs, thinking about the best means of escape. Then he knows.

"You tell me about yourself," he says.

And these are magic words. She was never that interested in knowing about him; she was just waiting for the turnabout. She tells him about the shop, with her dead-end job and her lecherous boss; she tells him about her ailing mother and her distant father and her brother, run off to join the army years ago and never returned. He eats his pie, and then the ice cream, as she talks about Bakersfield with an unexpected and fierce pride, and then she talks about her numerous attempts at escape.

"How do you do it?" she says. "How do you get away?"

"You just go, I guess," he says.

"Just like that? Really?"

He shrugs.

"Maybe if you can't just go," he says, "you might have a better reason than you think to stay."

She's looking at him so intently he wonders if she's noticing his makeup. His own self-consciousness is alarming. Is he a fake, or does she see him at his most real?

"Sis, you better get back to the shop," the waitress says from down the counter.

Nancy takes in a breath. "You're a good man," she says. "One of my favorites. I'm glad I met you."

She rises from her stool as if one condemned, and then fumbles through her purse to find money to leave on the counter. "If only life was like the movies, right?" she says.

The drive home from Bakersfield proves unsettling. The makeup has begun to dissolve in the sweat of a late afternoon, there's no air conditioning in the car, and the glare is in his eyes. More to his chagrin is the sense that this form of play-acting is about trying to see what he'd really have been. His mumbling father, rarely home and silent when he was, the weight of the world no different than Nancy's, just rainier.

A green truck passes him on the long dusty road. Flatlands to both sides, and he thinks of the crop-dusting scene with Hitch. *Was it out here somewhere?* He'd been chauffeured out and had barely paid attention that day, focused as he was on the script and the scene. It was easy to miss the world rolling right by.

On a county road, where a sign announces the approach to another roadside town. *Entering Weedpatch California.* Whoever named the place had to have had a sense of humor. Or maybe exasperation. Mobile homes shoulder up against the road, and then long expanses of dry alkalized land. A mangy dog, its tail straight up, trotting off to somewhere. The places he barely knows and the people he has long been insulated from. Somewhere ahead, this road will meet the highway, and then a wider one, which will sweep back into the city, making the final passage as sterile as a sluice of fresh water.

1935

HOW DESPERATELY WE KEEN to unearth the dead! And how complicated when they rise!

He'd found himself in the early years in Hollywood wondering what his long-dead mother might think of him, the awkwardly loved child now unabashedly loved by the masses. Each new picture he made seemed as if more altitude in an unbroken ascent. Each new height pulled him further from the crowd, and made him that much more the rara avis. The stage had only edged him up by inches, but the movies paintbrushed him across the sky. Typecast as he was as a pantomimist and comic presence, it hastened his rise as scores of somber young men were passed over.

He was now living in a sizable house, sharing quarters on West Live Oak Drive with Randy Scott, a man making his own surge at film fame. The house was white against the azure sky and with the Griffith Observatory off in the heights. They had a terrace and they sunned themselves into cast bronze. Young, handsome, and outwardly carefree men, studio favorites who graced the pages of movie magazines. Life was an ever-rising swell of riches as he entered his thirties.

Play it smaller. It was one of the first things he'd been told when he arrived in Hollywood, and he'd fought the opposite urges all his life. He'd been raised on the boards and that was the way they did it.

"Think of the myopic old fellow in the last row," Pender would always say. "Let him get his shilling's worth, too."

So that meant learning to display like a puff adder, up on the balls of the feet for another half inch, arms spread wide and the voice booming. Head turns, double takes, alley-oops, lurches and twists, shudders and shakes, all to make caricatures of normal movement. Pender had them practice three-step stage whispers: the leaning in, the tilting head, the hand to the mouth to direct the raspy sotto voce. And, if the receiver of such confidences, the throwing back of shoulders, the exploding of the hands, the dropping of the mouth, all intended to express the surprise and drama of the transmission and reception.

Arch got bigger and bigger as he went, first with the adolescent growth spurt, then his stilts. His voice boomed. Bigness became him. Early on, in the picture business, it was just more pantomiming. There was never a question of it being comedy. It was what he knew, how he was trained, and where his impulses took him. He had no need for pathos; he'd been running away from it for too many years. Pathos was what he did when he wasn't onstage, or in front of a camera. When he got his first big part, opposite Mae West, his default was still to please the myopic. And Mae's entire oeuvre already seemed to do just that, spiritually and anatomically. Silent movies had rewarded overstatement, and once she got to talk it only got bigger. But the director, Sherman, quietly reined Arch in for particular scenes, saying softly, "Don't move, boy, don't move." Then, "And now . . . move . . ." Arch learned that holding his ground made the kinetic interludes more forceful. But holding his ground felt like disappearing, the way he had to when he played minor roles and was itching for his brief moments.

But restraining himself was paying off. He was learning to listen, and cede the shot, knowing he made it more interesting by being there.

Despite all, it seemed a time of walking dead. The Depression wasn't breaking; it was getting worse as he got richer. Even in the California sun, the poor were everywhere, streaming in from the dust-bound farmlands, skeletal as they sat stunned in the golden light. A Hooverville sprung up in Watts, tent after tent, upward of a thousand people. Out in his new Duesenberg roadster, he'd sometimes pass old cars stripped of their engines and slowly pulled by underfed horses. Winter rains swept in and lashed the rickety settlements, sowing further desperation. And then one day the field would be clear, the settlement razed and its occupants scattered to the winds.

Rains reminded him, always, of Bristol, and of his father, from whom he rarely heard. Elias Leach was living with a woman and Arch saw that life in shades of gray, all colorless and steely and immutable. A man to be largely forgotten, as the memory of young Arch was also fading. Then the telegram: His father had drunk himself to death, alcohol poisoning on an otherwise unremarkable day of an unremarkable life. The crescendo of a flattened life on the bottle. A request for a return, to settle the old man's affairs.

The Acrobat put the telegram down, sat at the end of his bed, and attempted to weep. But nothing came. He was now without family, and the notion of Arch himself was becoming displaced by this new person he was, this slick fellow named Cary, this charmer, always elbowing his way in.

Marriage had not been on his mind, but it most certainly had been on the studio's. As had changing his name. They'd told him nearly upon his arrival that "Archie Leach" wouldn't do at all. He and Fay Wray, who was getting ready to shoot a picture with a very large gorilla, came up with "Cary Lockwood" —the name of his character in *Nikki*, the play they'd done together back in New York. The studio didn't like all those syllables. Someone had a list of last names and began reading them off. When it got to "Grant," the casting man said, "That'll work."

"Should we arrange a baptism?" the Acrobat had said, to no reaction.

But everybody found they were being changed. Duke Morrison became John Wayne. Inexplicably, Frank Cooper became Gary Cooper, acquiring a syllable. Fay Wray, who had the fortune of two monosyllabic names (although her middle and last; her real first name was Vina), was ordered to be a blonde. Merian Cooper was running RKO and he made these decisions.

Cooper was a hard case. This was a man who in his military career had chased Pancho Villa across Mexico, flown a bomber during the Great War, and escaped from a Soviet prisoner-of-war camp. After that, he moved into the movie business. Now he'd come up with the idea for *King Kong*.

"Clearly autobiographical," the Acrobat observed to Fay. Merian Cooper made him inexplicably nervous. Cooper worked for Howard Hughes, on paper, but even Hughes seemed intimidated by him. The man exuded a masculinity that seemed both cartoonishly overplayed yet completely backed up by exploits the Acrobat could only hope to perform onscreen. So when word came down from Cooper's office some time later, delivered by

Cooper's people but not Cooper himself, he was attentive.

"Mr. Cooper says you need to think about getting married soon," Cooper's man had quietly said. "Otherwise, people might start thinking you're a queer."

The shock was palpable. Why would that have occurred to them? Was Merian Cooper up there in his office giving this serious thought? For the first time, he was worried about the easy ascent of his career. He'd not thought of himself as the marrying type, but now, like a bolt, he was.

That led to the urgency of an employer needing to fill a vacancy. He'd just been in a small part in *Blonde Venus* with Marlene Dietrich, a film in which his character approaches her after he sees her in a show. The night of the premiere, he was approached by Virginia, and he was well primed to see the very best in her. She was a rising star in her own right. And she was exquisite. But this wasn't about love.

She'd played the blind innocent opposite Chaplin in *City Lights*. It turned out she was neither blind nor innocent. She was every bit the careerist as he; she seemed to watch him with a penetrating understanding of exactly who he was. This had unnerved him. He'd been trying to obscure who he really was for some time. Without a word, she made him feel acutely aware of being a pale boy with a sad life. He was no war hero or swashbuckler. He felt as if she would leave him at any moment, and so he became increasingly possessive of his new trophy. She'd left him after seven months anyway, divorced not long after.

One afternoon toward the end of the marriage, he entered the Brown Derby. He'd come to love that transition when the heat of the midday sun rising off the North Vine Street pavement gave way to the cool and darkened hush of this place. The rows of silver-enframed caricatures on the wall depicted celebrities, some of whom were now familiar friends. He hoped that one day his own image would join them. But for now, admission was enough. Not everybody got through that door. He was awaiting Virginia, who was at the studio and naturally late. She was getting ready to go off to England to make a picture, and he knew the other side of that wasn't going to include him. But, ensconced in his red-leather booth with a gin martini, he was happy to just be.

This was the migration, from being let into places where he could gawk at stars, to being seated prominently to be gawked at. His booth was a middling spot, where people seated there were either rising or falling. He had no doubt of his own direction. He was young, and there was time.

He glanced toward the door, as if to will Virginia's arrival and to be done with the marriage, but all was quiet. But behind him he could hear a voice that seemed a notch too high in volume, but oddly familiar. He couldn't hear words so much as tone, but he turned and there he was: Fairbanks.

A decade and a half since he'd seen him on the deck of the RMS *Olympic*. The hairline had receded, and the pencil mustache was flecked with gray. Fairbanks was now long separated from Pickford, who had stayed on up at the mansion. The Acrobat had followed this with great interest, and sadness. Now, in front of him, Fairbanks wavered unsteadily on his feet, waiting for the woman whom he was with to gather herself. He was clearly drunk; the cigarette in his mouth seemed as if permanently fixed.

The talkies had not been a success for Fairbanks. As Sennwald in the *New York Times* had said, "The microphone is ruthlessly unkind to him." And in that last picture before he retired the previous year, *The Private Life of Don Juan*, Fairbanks had exhibited in his swordfights and derring-do the unmistakable creaks and stiffness of rapid aging. The Acrobat had sat in the theater feeling sorry for a man he'd once seen as a god. The man, here in front of him now, was softly huffing behind his cigarette, looking irritated. He turned to the woman.

"Come now, Silky dear, we must be getting along."

"Right there," she said, in a rather queenly London accent of the type infrequently heard in Bristol. This was Lady Ashley, the woman who had famously decoupled Pickfair. Fairbanks stood there, waiting, and no one else seemed to be noticing.

Up the Acrobat sprang from his booth. Fairbanks seemed startled in a way he never was when rogues and ne'er-do-wells tried to ambush him onscreen.

"I just wanted to say hello, Mr. Fairbanks." The great man stood dumbly; this was off-script for the Brown Derby's carefully wrought conventions.

"We've met before, many years ago . . ."

Fairbanks nodded, waiting for more.

". . . on the *Olympic*. I was coming to America for the very first time."

"And now you're at the Derby," Fairbanks finally said. "I can't confess to knowing you. Should I?"

"I was just a boy. You showed me kindness. I always appreciated that."

"My pleasure, of course," Fairbanks said. "But should I know you now? You're here, after all."

"Well, you might have seen me here and there."

"Well done, then! I hardly ever go to the pictures anymore, though . . ."

He looked as if he would continue, but then he bent over, overcome by a guttural cough. A deep rattling that seemed to go on and on. The woman had come up behind him and laid her gloved hand across his shoulder blade.

Fairbanks took his cigarette from his lips, and with the

other hand he put his handkerchief over his mouth, bringing up something that sounded awful.

"Really must run now," he said nearly in a whisper. With a nod, he was off, and as the Acrobat refocused, he saw almost everyone in the Derby looking over, and not with any visible appreciation.

In the interlude from when that telegram arrived on the first of December, and when he departed to bury his father, the Acrobat tried to understand the old man a bit better. His father drinking himself to death was no surprise at all, but very much a shock. It seemed the man had tried to kill himself off in every conceivable way, but had failed as miserably as he had at most other things. Who knew this would be his one real success?

A month later, he was sitting in the solicitor's office going over the vestiges of a life. The little that Elias had saved (even after the gifts of money from his Hollywood son) would go to the "widow," the woman his father had never married but with whom they'd had a son, a half brother he barely knew. Combing over the ruins: the meager bank account, the paltry possessions. Another glimpse of whom Archie might have otherwise become, had he minded his father, played it safe, and presumed a modest life. He'd have been a pasty-skinned presser in old Bristol, slowly drinking himself to death in some dingy pub in Horfield.

Across the desk, the solicitor was taking it in: the prodigal son, thirty-one and an American film star, his California suntan offset by the cashmere overcoat and the foulard tie in bright colors, like a tropical bird loose in the gray dirge of winter. The Acrobat came back out of his mind's wandering and fixed on the man's gaze.

"Now, then," the solicitor said. "We must discuss your mother."

"What about my mother?" the Acrobat said.

"Well, I'd imagine you'll be assuming care for her . . ."

The Acrobat went silent for a measure.

"I've never actually seen her grave, you know. But, whatever the cost."

Now it was the solicitor's turn at silence.

"Your mother," he said again, more evenly.

"Right."

"Are you going to take care of her, moving forward? The cost is neither easy nor dear. Your father afforded it on his wages."

"What in God's name is there to pay for?"

"Food, lodging, treatment, medical care . . ."

Again, the head swirling; the Acrobat transported back to the inside of a Penderesque tumble.

"My mother is dead twenty years."

"I don't know who you've been speaking to, sir, but your mother is and always has been alive. She's been committed all these years at the asylum at Fishponds. Did someone tell you she was dead?"

Of course, no one actually had. At least not in those words. His mother had simply gone away and never come back. His father had stopped mentioning her; Arch had stopped asking. When someone mentioned she was "gone," it had always rung in his mind like the euphemistic peal of a funeral bell. After twenty years, he'd come to certain obvious assumptions, which were now exploding inside his skull.

1959

THE SCRIPTS COME ONE after another. They pile up on the table in his bungalow on the studio lot, the endless gamble of his time and talents, a future that can rest on these choices. He's learned to spot within ten pages whether it's a role he can see himself in; some he reads to the end even when he's determined he either shouldn't do the picture or can't do it.

But the reading is the reading. There's no romance to it, unless you're Marilyn Monroe, who is constantly photographed reading scripts in various sexy poses, as if the fact of her reading was a surprise. But he'd worked with her in *Monkey Business* and he knew what she brought to the table; the dumb-blonde act was as much an act as his highborn man. She was constantly recommending books to him that he'd never heard of and never had time to read. But there she was in the magazines, lingering over a script as if this was oxymoronic. He'd said to her, "People are surprised how little education I actually have." She had said, "People seem surprised I have any at all." They both had to make up for that lack of schooling, but the difference was he'd chosen to quit the minute he could. The fact that she'd gotten further than he before dropping out didn't mean she'd wanted to. She read and read; she went to the Actors Studio to study the Method but never seemed to use it in her pictures. Now she's married to Arthur Miller, and he can't imagine those high-minded conversations. He's heard some whispers that Miller's been writing a big screenplay for her that will change her life.

He, with his truncated education and limited patience, believes he reads a picture the way someone in the audience would watch it: with a need for things to happen. On he reads, dividing the piles on his desk into In and Out piles in which the In pile seems taller every time he walks into the room.

He's already committed to two new pictures after this year; he's looking at 1963 at the earliest. Then after that, he'll be sixty.

The script at hand is set in Paris, and it's clear it would be filmed on location. Not so bad, then. In it, he would play a charming man of mysterious means who in the story seems to take on many identities. Right up his alley. And the love interest would be a charming young woman he must help escape a group of murderous men who'd been in cahoots with her recently murdered husband.

And there he worries. The character of the girl, Regina, tracks young. And he'd heard through channels that they have Audrey Hepburn in mind. An age difference of twenty-five years. That's becoming more problematic. She was in *Funny Face* with Fred Astaire a couple of years ago and he'd felt a pang of worry about their scripted attraction. Did people really believe it anymore?

On the set again, he sees Scotty smoking a cigarette outside the stage door. Scotty holds out the pack and the Acrobat takes one, then accepts Scotty's lighter.

"Thought you were quitting these things," Scotty says.

"I'm just getting into character."

"Your character smokes in a submarine?"

"Only off-camera."

"I didn't realize you ever got out of character."

"Well, I did back in fifty-two. Retired for a few months and was beside myself with boredom."

"Funny, most people in this business would rather die with their makeup on."

"How did you ever find yourself here, Scotty? Working in the pictures."

"I grew up over in Yorba Linda, back when that was all just orange groves and celery fields. My family had just come from Nova Scotia. I guess I was going to be a farmhand, but then the war started."

"You fought in the Great War?"

"Didn't everybody?"

"I suppose they did, if they were old enough."

"So when I got back here, the pictures were just really

starting up. They were looking for strong boys who could carry heavy things. It sounded harder than farming, but it paid better. In time, they taught me carpentry, then electrical. I picked it all up pretty quickly. There was always demand for workers. Pretty soon, pictures were the biggest thing in this damned town. And that's the story."

"I take it you've been dealing with people like me for a long time."

"Oh, I've been around people like you forever. You're not such a bad lot. Once I understand how busted-up needy you all are, I stopped being resentful. Actors are actors, with all the warts you can't bear people seeing. I've had problems with very few stars."

"Who were the few you did have problems with?"

Besides yourself? The only one I really had friction with was Buster Keaton."

"Why, what did Keaton ever do to you?"

"He was loony, Boss. He'd make us rework the set ten times over until it satisfied him. I was the foreman, so I had to speak up. He'd work us to the bone for nothing, trying to get it right. He was drinking heavy then, though. He knew he was losing it, and it was making him crazy. The doctors tried putting him in a straitjacket, but Houdini had taught him how to escape one, so he kept getting away."

"Drinking gets the best of them, doesn't it?"

"Let me tell you, John Gilbert used to breathe fire. But what killed him was that nasal voice of his. When the silent pictures ended, so did he. Dead by his midthirties."

"You've known them all, haven't you?"

"No, but I've known an awful lot."

"And will I just be another story for you to tell?"

"Nah, Boss, I'll just be one for you to tell."

"That's true."

They both finish their cigarettes, and then Scotty says, "I better get back to it."

"Scotty, do you ever form an opinion of the pictures you're working on, watching them being shot?"

"Sometimes you can tell, Boss, but sometimes you can't. I worked on *Public Enemy*, and that was something. Everybody knew it. And the cowboy pictures—you almost can't go wrong. But the ones that weren't so good, you probably wouldn't remember."

"This picture is pretty awful, isn't it?"

"I've been wrong before, Boss, so I'll keep my opinion to myself. But it's interesting that you're asking me."

"Maybe it's time for me to get out of the business."

"Interesting that you're thinking that, too. But the difference between you and me is, you're rich enough to have a choice."

He's stopped by the bungalow on the studio lot to check his phone messages. James, the publicist from Key West, has left an urgent message. He's suggested there's a problem developing. The Acrobat's lawyer, Stanley, is now holding on the line.

"Stanley, is everything all right?"

"The *New York Herald Tribune* is going to run Joe Hyams's series about you, starting in the morning," Stanley says. "Apparently you went on at some length about this drug use of yours. Sounds as if it wasn't just a slip of the tongue."

"First of all, it's a prescribed *treatment*. And you need to stop that from happening, Stanley. I never told him he could use that."

"He's saying you let Lionel Crane at the London *Daily Mirror* use the material, and that it's fair game now."

"I hardly think so! I have no idea what's being printed in London. And nobody reads the *Daily Mirror* anyway! I also don't want this published in America. That series needs to be stopped."

"Why did you even talk to reporters about this?"

"It was on my mind. So I did."

"Hitch is very concerned," Stanley says. "*North by Northwest* opens in seven weeks."

"Can you get Hyams on the phone for me?"

"I'm not sure that's a good idea."

"I insist. I'll get this squared away."

"All right, then," Stanley said, and none too enthused.

But inside of an hour later, the phone rings and it's Hyams.

"Well, Joe, you need to pull this series I'm just now hearing about."

"I can't see that happening, sir. They'll be running the presses in a few hours. It's six o'clock back east. Everything is already Linotyped."

"I told you I'd let you know when you could publish this."

"I've already been scooped by the London paper, so it's all fair game now. I'm sorry."

"But you simply must pull that series!"

Hyams pauses, then says, "You probably have no idea what it would cost the *Herald Tribune* to reset the pages on deadline. I'm not going to ask them to do that."

"I'll get back to you," the Acrobat says, hanging up. He redials Stanley and says, "I'm going to deny I ever spoke to him."

Now it's Stanley pausing. "I'm not sure if that's a good idea."

"Not only did I not give him permission, but *Look* magazine has now offered a hefty price to me to relate my story. I could choose to talk about it there. If I'm going to discuss the Treatment, why would I give it away to the *Herald Tribune* for nothing?"

Stanley remains silent.

"Stanley, here's what to do. Release a statement from me denying I ever spoke to the man."

"Maybe think about that for a little bit," Stanley said.

"Please, Stanley, I insist. This is the best way to handle things. The last thing I want is this fellow thinking he can speak for me."

"I doubt he's going to like that."

"And why should I be remotely concerned with what a reporter does and doesn't like?"

"I don't know what to tell you to do," Stanley says. "I don't know why you ever talked to the press about this at all. Psychiatric treatments. Hallucinatory drugs! It's probably going to sink the picture. And if it sinks this picture, it will sink the next one, and it's all going to end up costing you . . ."

Beginnings

SEE A MAN EMERGING *from the steam of the pressing table; the endless, Sisyphean life of someone given few chances. It's the early years of the century, and this job is better than the alternatives. Twelve hours on his feet, smoothing the newly made clothes and swapping hot irons as if a juggler. Tending the flats, keeping them clean from staining the shirts, hot enough but not to scorch, all of them on the edge of the stove ready for their boxes to be filled with the glowing coals he must watch and tend. Rolled-up sleeves and his short necktie pushed into his shirt's placket to keep it out of the way. His collar rimed with sweat and his toes numbing in his shoes. For a man who has done this now for two decades, it is automatic, precise but yet mindless, careful but yet nearly unconscious. Each sharp crease is a continuation of a perfection hardly noticed. It is only in his failure that the work is noted at all.*

This man in the pub now, stooped over his stout in a night's exhaustion, but come to life, a personality risen out of the automaton of the pressing room. In these hours between work and sleep he can assert himself among those with like minds and like lots in life. A place where a pint can be had for a penny and a farthing, and where the newspapers trade hands among them and the arguments can ensue, rarely in anger and never put to test. Wives at home keeping pots warm, but no mind; the oppressive heat of the pressing room gives way to the welcome heat of some small bit of camaraderie he can find.

Then home, to the flinty wife and the shrinking child, to glumly eat the stew put him front of him by his glum woman, and the boy at the edge of the table, dressed for bed. It's the same life he knew in his own childhood.

He looks at the boy, who sits with eyes cast down. The man considers this. He's never mistreated the boy; he's never been harsh with him. While his wife has receded into her own darker places after the death of the first child, the man had to get on with things. No room for sorrow in his days. No time for falling to pieces. No one's going to be worried for him. He's nobody special and children die.

But the other side of that is the fear. He has kept this child, the living boy, at a far greater distance than the one he mourns. The man has given the living son everything while giving him nothing. The boy doesn't know anything different, of course; he knows nothing different than the way the man himself was brought up. The boy sits with eyes downcast, because he either wants something or he simply feels nothing at all, that he is only acting out his part in a story no one really believes in.

The man puts his spoon on the table and looks at the boy until the boy looks up at him. The thread to the dead child is unmistakable but he forces himself not to look away.

"A mate told me there's a good show at the Empire this week," he *says. "Would you fancy I took you?"*

The boy's eyes widen a bit, and he sits up straighter, as if a trick is being played upon him.

"We could go tomorrow night, if you'd like."

The boy nods, as if to say it out loud would be overstepping. And then he nods once again.

1939

THE PICTURES. THE PLACE where he'd discovered, as a boy in a dark theater, that his parents could smile, that they could actually laugh, that they could somehow shed the weight of their days, if only for the briefest interludes.

The Pictures, where he had found refuge as a lone boy sitting in a hard-bought seat.

The Pictures, which he'd studied as if ancient texts filled with wisdom and guidance. The comedies like bromides for living a happy, weightless life; the lesson that almost anything can be laughed at if you just try.

The Pictures, the place he schemed and strove to enter, to find himself on that side of the projection, to be on the watched world of excitement and risk and adventure. He wanted so badly, always to get there. And now he had.

The 1930s, his means of ascent, were nigh over. He'd entered the decade as a boy; he'd exit as a star.

But now another big war was brewing. There were men his age, thirty-five now, already enlisting in Britain. Technically, and despite all evidence to the contrary, he was still a subject of the Crown. As with his carefully wrought accent, the lines had blurred, and he was from nowhere and everywhere. He'd been living in the States for nearly two decades, but his passport was still British and his name was still Archibald Alec Leach. But he, or at least his alter ego, was American in every way he could imagine, and America wasn't in the war.

He'd come to love many things American. One such thing was baseball. The fun was in joining Randy or maybe Gary Cooper for Los Angeles Angels games at Wrigley Field, down in South L.A. The Americanness of it was one draw, but the neat clarity of the field, and the actions, had a tidiness that suited him, wherever that came from. From his father the devotion to sharp creases and unwrinkled collars, even as the man's life was otherwise lived so sloppily. But the Acrobat thought that baseball also fit Los Angeles, with its calibrated cartography of clean streets and neat neighborhoods and its sharp etching of light and dark. Old Bristol's rheumy shadings were always indistinct.

As the Depression gave way to the approaching clouds of another war, the Acrobat's fates were only blue skies. He seemed to be suddenly doing pictures with animals: There was the fox terrier, the leopard, and then the elephant. He was game. Three jobs in a row; he was getting typecast as "the human." But comedy became him and he didn't fight it. He seemed best when his role was to be lightly amused, and therefore amusing.

And he now played Americans, not the Brits he'd started out as. His accent was now indistinguishable aristocracy, not far off from Kate Hepburn's Connecticutese. They'd done *Bringing Up Baby* last year, and while it wasn't a complete flop, it melded them further. Hepburn was a like soul, he thought, despite her regal bearing. After they first met, making *Sylvia Scarlett* in 1935, she had said to him, "You should really meet my father. He's very concerned about venereal disease." Then she laughed at his expression. "Use that face in the picture," she said. Her father was a prominent doctor, she explained, and the founder of the New England Social Hygiene Association. In time, he realized he was picking up some of her speech patterns during the filming. She, athletic as she was, seemed to pick up a bit of his vaudeville jaunt.

He had fooled them all until he wasn't fooling them. He was now who he was. The name on his passport felt like sleight-of-hand. A charmed life, excluding the mysteries of marriage: Since the split with Virginia, he wasn't sure he wanted to reenter that particular institution. But, having removed his mother from another kind of institution, and having installed her in a small house with the proper care, he was still worried. *Would Britain fall as Herr Hitler blustered and bellowed? Should I have gotten her out?*

Her letters came regularly. Despite their renewed relationship, the arrival of each new missive had the feeling of someone speaking from the grave. The thoughts were cheerful and larded with praise, always addressed in careful hand to Mr. Archibald Leach; she seemed to want for very little and spoke not at all about whatever ordeals she'd withstood. He had taken her out of a bad place but perpetually felt as if he wasn't doing enough. And the whole buried history of what had happened made him struggle to try to remember his father fondly.

The studio asked him to pose for pictures. With Randy. They said yes. They were sharing the beach house in Santa Monica now, which they'd dubbed "Bachelor Hall." Randy had just been divorced from Marion duPont. But even married, she'd mostly stayed back in North Carolina, while he stayed mostly in Santa Monica. Randy wasn't having any trouble being single again, and seemed quite happy to resurrect the living arrangement they'd shared in the old Los Feliz house. Here on the beach, they had a cook and a housekeeper and a pool in the back, where they convened in the mornings to drink orange juice and take their morning sun and dive into still water.

The arrangement suited the Acrobat nicely. He'd lived alone enough as a lonely boy in the little house off Gloucester Road; Randy was the perfect man with whom to share the postdivorce bachelor life. The Acrobat had satisfied the studio's need to show he was marriageable, and now that was done with. In Hollywood, being divorced was unremarkable. Now he and Randy were reunited on the seashore, having both become bona fide stars. And Leo McCarey had just sent a script over for a film he wanted them both to star in: *My Favorite Wife*, it was called. He didn't know who the wife was supposed to be, but it read funny.

The photographer arrived after lunchtime, intent on using the golden light of the afternoon sun over the Pacific. He brought two assistants and many cases of lights and paraphernalia, which they erected so that the house had become as familiar as a soundstage. The Acrobat and Randy knew the roles they were to play: carefree young stars, living the magic life that stars live. Why this should have been of interest to people in the midst of the Depression was confounding, but Selznick, now the boss at RKO, said it "bucked people up."

Randy was in his tennis whites, as if he'd just bounded off the court. The Acrobat had white on as well, and the photographer said, by way of lightening the proceedings, "Don't you boys look virginal!"

"Shall we change, then?" Randy asked.

"It's fine, it's fine." The photographer, clearly another old studio hand who'd long since stopped being impressed, shrugged and said, "It's what you chose, so stay with that. You can put on swimsuits later."

The photographer told them what to do and where to do it: cooking together in the kitchen; sitting like a fusty old couple in the living-room easy chairs; out on the beach looking hale and happy. The Acrobat knew the movie magazines loved that kind of thing, and that the readership was almost all women. Two handsome fellows with domestic sensibilities seemed the order of the day.

In the kitchen, the Acrobat said, "How about a shot of me wagging my finger at him about leaving dirty dishes in the sink?"

"Nag, nag, nag," Randy said, but the photographer only stared at them. To Randy, it was all horsing around.

When the photographs came out a few weeks later, the usual people posited the usual innuendo. The gossip columnists, and in particular the execrable Hedda Hopper, raised their faux outrage, knowing it made for good copy and that was all that mattered. *Why are these men living together this way?* He doubted any of the columnists really believed any of it. Hedda wielded power, to be sure, but she could also go to hell.

But after the photos, it seemed, there was a more embedded suspicion. As if a friendship, of any order, was unnatural.

The fact was, he loved Randy. Their six-year age difference was profound. Randy had fought in a war and he had come to Hollywood earlier, and learned its particular form of engagement. He was a mentor and a brother and a confidant.

The Acrobat, once brotherless and adrift, cleaving to Randy, the man from the bustling brood of children and fully clear on what home was. As the Acrobat had spent his life avoiding the silence of an empty house, Randy's pedigree was a portable wealth. He could live in the noise and bustle of people at home, and if there was none he was likely to create it himself. The stream of friends to Bachelor Hall was steady. Noel Coward and

David Niven were similarly sharing a house just down the beach, soon enough dubbed "Cirrhosis by the Sea" in honor of their fondness for bottomless dry martinis.

Bachelor Hall focused on tanning and swimming and boisterous chat, and the stream of girls and the various male acquaintances trailing the girls like suckerfish attaching to the shark's hide.

But Bachelor Hall, like bachelorhood, was transitory. He'd been divorced from Virginia, but had nearly married several others, perhaps impetuously so, and was feeling the antsiness of being a man without a woman. For events and appearances, he was always with a companion, and some were finding a place in his affections. Phyllis Brooks, best known as the Ipana Toothpaste Girl, was quite lovely.

"I need to find a wife," he said to Randy as they sat by the pool.

"I can do without for a while myself," Randy said. "Once I make enough money, I'll find a girl and go back to North Carolina. But what kind of woman are you considering, old man?"

"I should go ahead marry Brooksie. She's a good friend. We get along splendidly. But I find myself hesitating."

"Just too good right here, is it?"

"Well, it's really not bad. And besides, her mother hates me and I feel likewise."

"Don't marry her, then."

"Well, people seem to be expecting it. One magazine is already calling Brooksie the next Mrs. Grant, which was news to me. It seems expected that I not be unattached."

Randy swirled his drink in its glass.

"It isn't those bloody photographs still bothering you, is it?"

"Randy, one must maintain an eye toward expectations."

"Your own? Or the will of our masters in the studio?"

"A little of both. Settle down, have children, and so on. With

Brooksie, they'd have wonderful teeth."

"Settle down like normal people do."

"Yes, like that."

"The problem is finding a normal person in Hollywood. We're an odd breed, really, aren't we?"

"Speak for yourself, Randolph. I crave the normal life."

"I'm not sure either of us has any real idea of what normal is anymore. We just mimic it in front of the camera. I think what you might be after is an extra-special normal."

"Yes, I take your point. If normal life is so marvelous, why is it that all our fans are trying to escape from it by going to the pictures?"

Then, a dinner party. He was seated next to Barbara Hutton, who had just been divorced from some dissolute count from someplace or another; she'd previously been divorced from a self-styled prince from an Eastern European backwater. That was the funny thing about rich Americans: They adored royalty all out of proportion. But tonight she was seated with a commoner, who had never despised the titled gentry but always had a healthy skepticism.

They'd been seated together with purpose; matchmaking was a Hollywood parlor game. The Acrobat didn't mind. And, once they got talking, she didn't seem a bad sort, despite all her money.

"Do you remember meeting me once before?" she asked, and he had already been reminded of this by their helpful hostess.

"Yes, on the *Normandie*, however could I forget the pleasure?"

"I thought you might have tried me. On the telephone."

"Oh, I normally communicate through telegrams only. Didn't you receive mine?"

She smiled and said, "Telegrams are never good news, in my

experience. I have my butler burn all incoming telegrams."

"I'm very sure you do."

He couldn't explain the ease at which she put him that night. People that wealthy rarely had a sense of humor. Randy's ex-wife, the duPont girl, had many fine qualities, but she was much too serious. Well bred, well educated, kind, engaging. Just not very funny. Not quick with the wit. It had not helped the marriage, Randy had observed.

"So what does the woman with everything do for fun?" the Acrobat now said.

"I wouldn't know. I've never heard of a woman who thinks she has everything. In fact, I'm currently without a regular escort."

"That's a story I've heard going around," he said, as he realized everyone up the table was eavesdropping on them.

1959

HE'S WAITNG FOR HIS limo just outside the soundstage, one afternoon. Just letting the sun warm his face—no chance squandered to deepen his tan—his eyes closed so that he sees a reddened darkness and feels just the lightest of air. When he hears the voice, it's almost as if out of the wail of a long-ago storm.

"Look at this clever poseur," the voice intones, as light as the breeze and as outback as ever.

The Acrobat opens his eyes to see the Aussie himself, someone he's mostly, and oddly, been able to avoid in this small town. He calls himself Orry-Kelly now, which the Acrobat found preposterous until he found out the man's actual name was Orry Kelly. It was "Jack" that had been the invention.

"My word, you've turned into an old man," the Acrobat says.

"And you've turned into a man at all."

"But as I look at you, I see that you are the old man you were always intended to be. Your face fits this better."

"Your face, on the other hand, remains as fey as I recall it. You know, I got Tony Curtis in a dress in *Some Like It Hot*. We can arrange a fitting if you like."

"Why, Jack, you're still just the old tout, aren't you?"

"Always. How is it I never got to dress you?"

"I have Edith Head for that."

"Our Edith. She outdid herself with the Riviera film. You looked sublime."

"Thank you."

"But you always wore clothes exceedingly well. Part of your secret to have shoulders like a mahogany clothes hanger. I may have undressed you once or twice, but I could have given Edith a run for her money with you, had I got a chance to."

"Maybe. And seriously, Jack, how's your health?"

"How does it look?"

"It looks like hell."

"The wages of sin, to be sure."

"And are we still drinking?"

"As enthusiastically as ever, we are."

"Rethink that, will you?"

"I always do, right before I pour another one. So if you don't at all mind, I already have you penciled in as a pallbearer."

"Me? Are you quite serious?"

"The more I think of the old times, the more I think of the happiness of it. We were nobodies living with our dreams, weren't we? Happy nobodies."

"Speak for yourself."

"I don't have big dreams anymore, Arch."

"Well, you already have two Oscars."

"And that's where the end is at a beginning."

"Funny thing is, Jack, I feel young. I still have lots of dreams yet to fulfill."

"You always did, Arch."

The car has eased to the curb. The driver comes around to open the door, and whatever either of them might say now has an audience neither of them wants. The Acrobat offers a courtly bow but does not extend his hand.

"We were so hungry, once," the Aussie says.

When he arrives home and settles in for a quiet night, the phone begins ringing almost immediately. He waits for someone to answer it, but it rings on and he realizes he's alone in the house. He picks up and it's his lawyer.

"Big problems," Stanley says. "That reporter, Joe Hyams? He's suing you for a half million dollars."

1943

WAR AND THE ABSURDITY of being so insulated from it. Jimmy Stewart flying bombers over Europe. Clark Gable a gunner in B-17s. Hank Fonda on a destroyer in the Pacific. Randy had already fought a war and had nothing to prove in this one, especially at forty-three years of age as the war began. But the Acrobat, now thirty-nine, was comfortably installed in a Pacific Palisades mansion called Westridge, married to the second-wealthiest woman in America. Only John Wayne was more of a sad spectacle, leading his troops to soundstage victories in scripted battles, then going to dinner afterward at his favorite steakhouse.

This was a state of deep discomfort, even snugged in comforts he had yet known. In his later thirties, he couldn't be expected to be fighting on some beach or flying a bomber, even though fellow actors only three or four years younger were. He missed the first war by being a shade too young, which he never had to apologize for. Now, he was a shade too old and feeling as if everyone was waiting for a mea culpa. That didn't feel fair. He'd tried to enlist! But going forward, as he then had, rapidly felt as if it were the greatest miscalculation in his life. He was enduring world hostilities as Barbara Hutton's husband.

They were living in a mansion staffed with a cadre of servants. He'd tried to count, and came up with twenty. Such a legion was something his new wife had always known, but he'd been working up to it. Hiring a cook and a driver was not what this was. Prying eyes, pricked ears, hovering sensibilities. His years at the beach house with Randy had been a celebration of their privacy, something movie stars especially needed. Barbara had never known true privacy; her version of being alone had a dozen people hovering over her. She treated them as nonpeople, but at every turn he saw faces quietly taking note, hearing all, watching.

"Don't worry," she told him. "They're trained not to listen."

"Yes, I'm sure they are."

That was inside the house. Outside, he was being laughed off as an opportunist. Which he was in many ways, but not in this particular way.

The long dining table, too kingly even for his elevated tastes. But Barbara, wife and presumptive queen, knew no other way. A favorite habit of his, eating dinner stretched out on the bed, had been met with appalled silence. Each meal here was laid on bone china and taken with sterling silver, all liquids ingested from crystal, as Barbara was doing now as the morning sun came yawning over the backside of the estate and lit up the tapestries. The elixir that launched her into each new day was Coca-Cola and vodka, and while he had never been averse to a drink, nine in the morning seemed a tad aggressive. Yet here he was, and possibly in love (or at least love of a kind).

Since his father had died of the drink, the Acrobat had resolutely limited his own libation. He mostly attached to champagne and the occasional gin. But he understood from his own case history that a night of excess sometimes desperately required a morning of drink, and Barbara never missed a night of excess. It was understood he had nothing to say about this. In sad fact, he enjoyed her more when she was in her moments just before the drunkenness had hit its apex, in the way skyrockets hang for that fraction of a second in their roar and glitter, before fizzling out and plunging back to earth. She could be very amusing in her cups, until she suddenly wasn't.

But this was morning. She busied herself with her crabmeat and crepes. As often was the case in the morning, she was hazed over. The dime-store princess; the American version of royalty she had pursued so relentlessly without fully realizing it. But right now, she probed the crabmeat with her fork, as if conducting an autopsy.

"Bright new day, my dear," he offered.

She looked up as if he were a stranger.

"A bit too bright, if you must know," she said.

So he was thirty-nine now, and she was thirty-one; he was ascendant and she was trying to outrun her image to the world as the child who inherited fifty million from the estate of her grandfather, Frank W. Woolworth. The asymmetry of that! The constellation of a thousand Main Street stores devoted to the simple desires of the American commoner, producing this young woman lost in the depths of her own riches.

Barbara had never known true adversity, other than of the most important kinds. Money was always there; happiness, rarely. But he understood. After all, his own mother had only disappeared. Barbara as a child had found her mother dead in their suite at the Plaza, and of the woman's own doing (poison), despite the stories fed to the press about an ear infection. What really killed Edna Woolworth was her husband's betrayals. When the Acrobat had finally found his long-presumed-dead mother, she'd been sitting in a room, looking surprised he ever presumed so. She'd just thought he wasn't interested in seeing her.

That first time, meeting Barbara on an ocean liner crossing the Atlantic, was very much an instance of two ships passing. He was in first class, regretfully signing autographs for young admirers and a few giggling matrons. And there she was, the Poor Little Rich Girl (as the tabloids had called her, in those same years when he was starving in New York and depending on the fickle patronage of the Aussie). But the Poor Little Rich Girl was grown up, and even richer, and in the aftermath of two ex-husbands. He'd at first offered wide berth.

And their marriage license: Archibald Leach and Barbara Reventlow. She was carrying the name of Number Two, the no-account count. But as they pronounced her "Mrs. Grant" that July of 1942, he couldn't help but think she had just wed a mirage. He hadn't fully realized he'd done the same.

And so now, a year and change later, he sat watching her picking at crabmeat and loathed his own predicament: He was never fully cut out to be royalty of any stripe. Around this house, he was the man in the emperor's new clothes. He was, at best, a parvenu. He resented the constant incursions of the servants, and he despised the joke the press had made of it all. He'd worked twenty years to make it on his own, and amass some wealth, and he'd pledged on his wedding day to never touch a cent of her fortune. Yet now he was being ridiculed as a bloody male gold digger.

"And how's that breakfast?" he said now.

"Divine, as it always is," she mumbled suspiciously.

"When I was a boy, we'd have herring and stirabout. We might have that some one of these mornings."

"Might we, now . . ."

"It's a sturdy meal. A meal of the people. Porridge and kippers! Something your grandfather Woolworth might have eaten for breakfast."

"My grandfather only took black coffee for breakfast."

"See, then?"

That afternoon, knocking on the door of what he still considered his own house. Randy answered, obviously alone. The Acrobat felt as if he might weep. The mechanics of arriving on his own front step like a lost soul had been predictably complicated: The fact that he had ridiculously thought he and Barbara would live at this beach house was now an object, and abject, demonstration of his own naïveté. He'd even bought out Randy's share, something his good friend had accepted with a silent aplomb. And then Barbara's refusal, and then the selling back to Randy, who now stood here at the door, tan, fit, smiling.

"Look at the sorry vagabond," Randy said, stepping back to let him in.

"You don't even know the half of it, my friend."

Randy motioned to him to sit. All the same furniture; nothing moved or replaced through the successive sales of the house to each other. Randy poured the customary gin and tonics, just as they had when, as a couple of handsome bachelors, they'd had their cocktail hour and waited for a wave of women to crash on their beach. The Acrobat sank into his familiar chair, and Randy said, "Hey, that's my chair now, son."

"It's all yours, and I miss it terribly," the Acrobat said. "It's the dilemma of wanting to change your life and also let it stay exactly the same."

"That's why we're actors, bub. We change who we are every three or four months and then we come home at night. Are you sure you're not being held against your will up there in Pacific Palisades?"

"I'm wondering why I ever agreed to it," the Acrobat said ruefully. "And to think the lawyers even gave me an escape clause."

He'd met with her lawyers in the months before the wedding, without her ever mentioning anything. A folded note on a silver tray from her butler, Charles; calls made to his own attorney, until he sat with three men, and with assorted others, in a conference room overlooking Wilshire Boulevard. His friend and agent of record, Frank Vincent, sat nearby. But the Acrobat always did his own negotiating.

The meeting was amid the busy shooting of *Arsenic and Old Lace* that late fall of 1941; a quick trip from the lot still feeling as harried as poor Mortimer Brewster with his crazy aunts.

Barbara's lawyer's name was Mattison. He was youngish and well-dressed, and he seemed to have a Mona Lisa smile that never precisely waxed or waned.

"So the thing is, in the interests of your limited time, is that you're British," Mattison said.

"An accident of birth, I assure you."

"Be that as it may, it's a big problem."

"There's very little I can do about that, is there?"

"But there most assuredly is. You're less British than you think you are, after living here for so long. Frankly, watching you in the pictures, I couldn't even quite pin you down. I'd guessed New York City, and more precisely the Upper East Side, and more precisely than that, East Seventy-Third Street. But it might have just as easily been Ceylon."

"And so how do I change the circumstance of my birth, then?"

"You don't. I'm not speaking of *then*, I'm speaking of this very moment. Because in point of legal fact you are Archibald Leach, subject of the Crown. And we can't possibly have that."

"Then what would you have?"

"That you become an American citizen as quickly as possible."

"Me? An *American*? I just can't see it." Like so many of his expatriate friends—Hitch, Niven, Olivier, Coward—he seemed to occupy a safe harbor by being a Brit in Hollywood. Giving that up felt like a risky prospect. Odder still, Barbara was an American who wasn't an American. She'd renounced her own citizenship when she married the count, becoming a Danish citizen so as to pay lower taxes. Now, the Nazis controlled the Danish banks and everybody was nervous.

"Thus an American became a Dane, then wants to marry a Brit, but now he needs to become an American?" the Acrobat said. "Do I have that all correct?"

"Because you're a British subject, and because war is on there, and because you are to be married to a woman of such wealth, there is growing certainty that some of her wealth that resides in Britain could be frozen there—because of your connection to it, if you were to marry."

"I don't even want anything from her," the Acrobat said. "I thought I already signed all those papers."

"It's more complicated than that," Mattison said. "They're afraid people are going to pull their money out of the economy if a German invasion is imminent. Which, of course, they will. Your wife-to-be, or more specifically the financial advisors to her—of which I am one—are ready to make that move, and you'd be the potential obstacle. On the other hand, if you were American, it would become much easier."

The Acrobat sat silently. They had made their calculations, and he was making his own.

"Is this marriage even a good idea?" he said.

Mattison pushed back a bit from the conference table.

"Practically speaking, I certainly don't think so."

"Why is that? Will I compromise her happiness?"

"My job is not to think about her happiness, it's to think about her assets."

"But does she think about her assets?"

"No, of course not. That's why she pays me."

"And I'm a liability, then . . ."

"In many ways, yes."

"You mean there's more than just this one way?"

Mattison nodded to a dark-haired man in a gray suit adorned with a carnation.

"You present several problems," the man said.

"And who might you be?"

"I'm Hannagan," he said, definitively.

"Well, give me just one more little hint."

"I'm the press agent."

"Ah, yes, and there it is. I presume, then, the problem is the press."

"It always is. And your possible wife-to-be . . ."

"Possible?"

"It hasn't happened yet, has it?"

"You sound doubtful."

"You just asked if it was a good idea."

"I suppose I did, Hannagan. Now tell me about another problem I hadn't even known I posed."

"The image problem, for your fiancée. She's terrified of the press. They've really beaten her up over the Denmark situation."

"I can see that. But as I understand it, her husband insisted!"

Hannagan nodded. "She just needs to rethink the habit of marrying ne'er-do-wells."

"Good Lord, hint taken! Am I in that crowd, in your view?"

"Only if the press decides you are."

"Why would they?"

"You're sitting out the war, and getting ready to marry wealth."

"I tried to enlist in the Royal Navy! Lord Lothian said to stay here and do what I'm doing. I'm donating my bloody earnings from *Arsenic* to the British Red Cross. Listen here, I've tried to do my bit, and so did Noel Coward and Cedric Hardwicke, we all tried . . ."

"Well, there's a fighting force that would strike fear in Hitler's heart," Hannagan said.

"Be nice, now, sir."

"Look," the attorney Mattison said, "if you want to marry the woman, you need to be American."

The Acrobat nodded his consent, but Mattison had more to say.

"It might also neaten things up to do away with all this Archibald Leach nonsense," the lawyer said. "It makes it look as if you're hiding something."

Now, sitting in his former house, he was regretting things.

"I had the bloody escape clause that day."

With his drink in hand, Randy said, "You were hoisted with your own petard."

"Is that supposed to mean something?"

"Sorry, bub, I forget you're a vaudevillian, not a Shakespearean."

"Why, have you been hanging around with Shakespeareans in my absence?"

"Sir, I'll remind you I was educated at the Woodberry Forest School."

"They made you go to school in the forest?"

"Hamlet," Randy finally said. "It's from Hamlet. Blown up with your own bomb, which I'll say, parenthetically, that I saw more than once during the Great War."

The Acrobat, indeed always hoisted into high dudgeon when life told him he had overreached. But a smiling Randy, swirling his drink as the waves pounded the beach, said, "Look at poor old Archie, back slumming with the common folk, here, now."

The Acrobat raised his glass. "Look at me, craving my time with the hoi polloi such as yourself."

"Can't run with the fast crowd, bub. They have their own ways."

"Yes, and they're having their ways at my house again, tonight."

He sat that afternoon with Randy, looking at the ocean. The man was a brother, a father figure of sorts, and a companion. In his years growing up, and in the years after that in the business, he'd found no confidant and friend as Randolph Scott was.

"You know what the problem is?" the Acrobat said. "It's that when I'm single I want to be married, and when I'm married I want to be single. When I'm alone I want the crowd, and when in the crowd I want my solitude."

"Shall I not rent out your room, then?"

"Well, I don't want to come back here and find some traveling salesman in there."

Randy looked over at him.

"And so you've decided?"

"I actually haven't decided anything. It just seems to be going there. I'm not married to a woman, I'm married to a household. I'm married to a queen and her court. And I may be the only one who isn't aware of his role."

"A failure of imagination," Randy said.

"Maybe so, maybe so. And on another note, I came to get something."

Randy hadn't thrown away the stilts. They were in the back of the attic, where they'd been since the move into the house. The Acrobat, sentimental about such things, had brought home this pair he'd come across in a prop room at the studio, and had on a few afternoons in the sun gotten up and showed his skills off for some of the ever-present girls who sat sunning themselves with their drinks in their hands. He found it was a balance that returned easily, almost muscle memory, and that walking three feet higher than the rest of the world had made him once feel, as a very young man, weightless, and free.

There they were: simple, the very simplest of devices, and in their neglect rimed with a coating of dust and beach sand. These were not the strapped-on stilts he wore in the shows, the so-called Chinese stilts covered by the long pant legs; these were rudimentary handhelds, with all four limbs taking part in the balancing. The foot plates were low enough to step onto easily, at least for someone who had gone much higher. That these were a touchstone to a simpler life would not have been what he expected.

Out on the patio, the Acrobat mounted them, and looked over the wall at the crashing waves across the wide Santa Monica beach. For the first time all day, things felt natural. He was back in his former life, mimicking what was gone. For the first time, he wasn't sure forward movement was the given he'd always presumed.

*   *   *

Committing to being American was, as it turned out, far less daunting than committing to legally being Cary Grant. It had always just been another role, inside which Archie Leach lurked, and laughed. He could, in his duality, both reap the spoils and maintain an amused distance. He was feeling it all the more in this strange marriage he'd entered. The ceremony had lasted four minutes, and the announcement of their marriage, presumably put out by Hannagan, ended by saying *Mr. Grant will enlist as soon as he puts his affairs in shape.* There was something odd about the wording. He read it like a code to be deciphered. But on its face the message was plain: He'd now be looking like a coward of two nationalities. Welcome to America!

He wondered within days of the wedding if it was worth it. Barbara was a fundamentally decent person who was hopelessly lost. Lost in her sedatives and her vodka, lost in her money, and especially lost in the coterie of hangers-on of which he hoped, desperately, he wasn't a member. There was a broken-down alcoholic former tennis professional named Dallaire, who just seemed always on the edges, drink in hand and rarely a racket to be seen, occupying a guest room and moving through the place like a haunting. She had an alcoholic cousin named Jimmy Donahue who would appear with his valet nearly holding him upright, and who had such an odd air about him that the Acrobat could barely look him in the eye. And there were the Europeans, whom he took to be fascists sitting out the war in America. They came and rarely went; they were guests who carried themselves as masters and mistresses of the estate. One who came and went was a young ski champion named Igor who seemed to need to borrow gas money. Another was a Bavarian couple who seemed to suggest they were in close accord with Herr Hitler and went on about the scourge of the lower classes while they took the free food. The Acrobat seemed, in fact, to be the odd fit.

He'd come home from Randy and she'd just gotten up from a nap and had a drink in her hand.

"Darling," he said, "I can't help but wonder who all these people are, and what they're doing here."

She looked up, utterly blank.

"Who?"

"These people, all of these people. I didn't marry them, I married you."

"These people are my life, my existence. I wouldn't know how to live without my friends."

"Friends? What I see are con artists, layabouts, and hangers-on."

"These are nobles, dear. And they've been driven from their own homes by this horrible unpleasantness in Europe. Where do you expect them to be?"

"Making their own way, maybe?"

"That's because you weren't raised in my world. This is how people such as myself live. Not everyone is as talented at profiting off the public as you are. But we all understand it's how you were raised."

"I wasn't exactly feral, my dear."

"I'm quite sure you weren't. I can only take your word for what you've told me."

"Yes, I have embroidered my own story, and now I'm doomed to live with it."

"Don't be so hard on yourself. You've caught on to things quite well."

Barbara took a bit of her drink and looked at him more squarely.

"And so, all those people will be here tonight, dear. Did you forget about my dinner party?"

"I haven't forgotten," he said. "But to my bottomless regret,

I'll need to be reading scripts in my bedroom tonight."

She looked up from her food and he realized how drunk she already was.

"But you're the main attraction!"

"I'm the sideshow, you're saying, profiting for your gallery."

"Everyone loves movie stars, dear, as difficult as you all may be."

"Then I'm terribly sorry I can't join you for dinner."

"Just come down to say hello, then."

"I probably won't have time."

"I'm going to insist, then. Please."

"This is really what you want?"

"It is."

"Well, for you, dear, your command is my command, for which you all shall receive a command performance."

Barbara's butler, Charles, was a seasoned veteran not only of the Great War but of Barbara's two previous marriages. Before the no-account count, there was the fake prince from Russia, dead already from driving way too fast in the company of a rather racy baroness. The Acrobat thought himself a bargain at any price after these two.

Charles seemed ill-fitted to California. No evidence existed that he'd ever availed himself of sunshine. In his practiced seriousness, this man knew his place and his duties, and gave no evidence of a family, or of an interest in anything beyond selfless service to Barbara. Charles was quiet, polite, and deferential, and no one made the Acrobat feel as fraudulent as Charles did. It was that sense of stiff-upper-lip forbearance, of attending to a man he probably saw as far beneath him. Bringing England to Hollywood seemed to be doing no one any good.

At five o'clock, Charles came up with a tray of supper as

Barbara's presumptive friends poured in downstairs for another overblown, overbudgeted dinner party. Cocktails began early with this set. Barbara was throwing away money trying to impress these louts, but for her there would be no running out of money. She had the terrible misfortune of having been born without need, hunger, or worry.

Charles placed the tray on the Acrobat's bedside with the kind of surgical arranging that spoke of his discomfort at indulging the Acrobat's penchant for dining upon the mattress, *manger sur le lit*, in a way not even a truly lowly Englishman would. No, this was worse: It was so very *American*. Charles stood back and looked at the silver serving tray with a blankness that finely calibrated itself as traceless seething disapproval.

"Sir," he said drily, "you'll be expected to appear in the dining room at seven."

"Fetch me my tails, then," the Acrobat said.

Seven o'clock. And so here came he, into the gathering, storming the palace though he was presumptive king, the stilts clomping across gleaming floors and priceless rugs, him threading himself through the artifacts of a strange life, the vases and paintings and statuettes. The tuxedo was paired with his tennis shoes, for better grip. He ducked under the chandelier and entered the dining room. Barbara was at the end of the long table, as always, and the guests all turned with the kind of frozen, vapid smiles he mostly associated with film producers.

"Hallo there, luvs and guvs," he shouted in his best imitation of Cockney. But it seemed what these people wanted, and so he gave it to them. But the reaction was something he was not accustomed to: dead silence.

"I was asked that I put on a show, so here I am, then," he said, walking the stilts around the edge of the dining table as everyone looked to Barbara for her reaction, which was not laughter, even feigned. Indeed, she was staring at her dinner plate.

"The lady of the house, how she loves her soirees. And I am nothing if not aiming to please!"

He began to tilt at such a velocity it seemed he would slam to the floor, but this was just a Pender feint. The sound of people sucking in breath to prepare themselves for the crash was exactly when he pulled out, leapfrogging the stilts back under himself, then standing tall. They were all in his thrall, in frozen inhalation the way people do just before the terrible thing happens. The showman's smile was automatic. Even in a foray to embarrass his wife and show his contempt for her friends, he was finding the unending need to put on a good show.

Down the table, a young woman suddenly shrieked with laughter she'd apparently been trying to hide. And the others, relieved of being the first, let themselves go. He felt now at cross purposes, as if they actually liked him, which was the last thing he sought.

Barbara, deadpanning, looked up at him.

"Are you drunk, dear?" she said.

"Funny thing is, I only act drunk when I'm sober!"

Barbara was the last not to laugh, and then she did, as forced as he'd ever seen. Just going along with the crowd. It wasn't funny to her, but she wasn't going to be the spoilsport among her friends.

The Acrobat was finished here.

"Just a quick tour and I'm off," he said. "I do three shows a day: breakfast, lunch, and dinner. And don't forget to tip poor Charles!"

As he turned, there was Charles, and for the first time, the man's eyes were on fire. The Acrobat thought the butler was going to try to knock him over—he recognized that base impulse rising from beneath the propriety—but the man's training seemed to override his impulses.

Through the foyer and down the hallway, happy for high ceilings, and still hearing only the confused cackles behind him. He knew that if his marriage was not over tonight, he should not fool himself. It was over nonetheless. He was, in the end, just a Pender boy, incorrigible to the very end.

Aquamarine

HE AND RANDY: SUSPENDED, *weightlessly, timelessly, joyously in the pastel rectangle of a swimming pool under that Santa Monica sun. Underwater, holding their breaths, turning themselves into slick sea creatures of a pair. Tan, lean, strong. Fraternal twins of a particular lineage. Above the surface, the sky is as deep blue as the ocean that lies so close and stretches so far. The pool is like a sample case of that greater and unknown world, a submersion into the slightest edges of the expanses into which they could venture.*

The sounds are insular, the feel of the warmed water amniotic. They are amphibians littorally masquerading as land beasts; they are dolphins sleek in their element among the unimaginative fish. They communicate in a way not understood by those who live above the surface.

They don't seem to need to breathe. They could stay under endlessly, it seems. The twists and turns through the water seem instinctual, and free. The pool seems both tightly contained and still roomy enough. Up above, he senses, people await their return.

Randy comes undulating through the water toward him, smiling the phosphorescent smile. He holds an arm straight out, hand grasping as if Neptune leading with his trident. The Acrobat answers in kind, kicking to move forward.

They are reaching out for each other's fingertips as if painted on the ceiling of the Sistine Chapel, but just as those fingertips touch they each pull back, and then surge upward for the surface. The air is all up there. They've been submerged too long. People above await; people worry.

1959

HE PACES IN HIS bungalow office at the studio lot, awaiting Joe Hyams's arrival. The journalist has arranged this after much negotiation, and the moment draws near. The Acrobat does some breathing exercises. This is a focused attempt to get into character, to get into the role called upon right now, which is a man relaxed and mostly amused.

The fallout from the *Herald Tribune* series has stunned him. After the release of his statement denying having ever spoken to Hyams, the reporter has now sued for defamation. Unheard of, really. In different times, that would have been career suicide— and may still be. The people who cover the movie business have been presumed to not want to alienate the studios, at any cost. One would have presumed Hyams would have quietly receded.

Instead, Hyams has filed a lawsuit for a half million dollars.

"Does he really believe that was the amount of the damage?" the Acrobat says on the phone to Stanley. "It feels like some kind of stunt, and it's all over the newspapers. Everyone is going to find out if this means the end of the man's career."

"Everyone is also going to find out if this will cost you half a million," Stanley says. "I wish you'd taken my advice."

"It's not as if I'm actually being caught in a lie, Stanley. I know I lied, and pretty much everyone else does. That's beside the point. Or it possibly is the point: It's the way it works."

"It's the way it's always worked, I agree with that."

"Louella Parsons has just written about all this. Listen to this: 'When I was a girl, things were different in the newspaper business.'"

"Yes, the studio arranged that," Stanley says.

But in the deposition, Stanley says, Hyams has produced the tape recording and a photo taken of them on the deck of the pink submarine, apparently by the studio's own set photographer. It was all so much bolder than one might expect of a journalist who depends on stars to give him the time of day. Meanwhile, poor James, the studio public relations man, has disappeared from the face of the earth, apparently avoiding a deposition of his own.

"Well, we need to make this go away," Stanley says, with a curl of gloom on his voice.

"Like we always make these things go away."

The Acrobat has insisted the meeting be on his territory, and alone. Maybe a bit of a reminder of who controls the town. But when Hyams comes through the door, with that same confident smile, it's clear the man is far from contrite.

"I hope you don't expect me to kiss your ring," the reporter says.

"A formal bow will do just fine," the Acrobat says, motioning for him to sit.

Hyams slumps onto the couch in the Acrobat's small office.

"Well, Mr. Hyams, I must admit this was the first I ever heard of a Hollywood newspaperman suing a Hollywood star. I would have thought it was a terrible idea."

"Well, I wasn't going to sit there and be called a liar."

"Frankly, I find that odd. We call you liars all the time! And quite often you are. Do you see what *Confidential* does to people?"

"I hope you're not comparing the *New York Herald Tribune* to *Confidential*."

"I suppose not."

"And I do understand the game around here. Your publicists drop a few tidbits that generate talk, then you deny it to protect yourselves. Or, for that matter, they drop lies that they wish were true and hope everybody believes it, then issue soft denials no one believes. So yes, I get it. You build your star power, but take no accountability."

"You sound as if you don't enjoy all this."

"Not true. It's a bit of fun being around here. Sure beats covering City Hall. But when you disavow something that big, and something that seems so improbable, you're trying to destroy my livelihood. 'Hyams fabricates a story about Cary Grant taking LSD.' That's a bridge too far. And frankly, the idea of you taking LSD is so preposterous people would assume I made it up."

"I'd think suing me might be what destroys anyone's livelihood."

"Hollywood is changing, sir. The world is changing."

"Yes, and I'm finding it's quite a problem."

Hyams then seems to gather himself and says, "My son has been getting bullied about this."

"Bullied? Over this?"

"At his school. Boys pushing him around and telling him his father's a liar. The kid is ten years old, sir!"

"Why would boys that age care about some minor spat like this?"

"Because their fathers work for the studio."

"Well, I certainly don't condone that!"

Hyams shakes his head, still smiling, but woefully. "But, see, that's how you people are. You stars. You're so goddamned high and mighty you don't think of anybody else."

"I'm not that way at all!"

"I bet you think that. And I bet that at some point in your life that would have been true."

"Now, Joe, see it from my position. You must understand that I have a lot of money tied up in these pictures. The publicists are concerned with the effect your articles will have. We can't have people deciding to watch television instead."

"And you sounded so convincing when you said LSD had made you see everything clearly . . ."

"Mr. Hyams, were you smiling just like that when you stormed the beaches?"

"That's amusing."

"Are you going to give me a karate chop now, sir?"

Hyams takes a breath.

"I was just joking, Joe."

"I'm not making a judgment on your LSD treatments. Whatever works, right? Such as my study of the martial arts. You may think of karate chops, but to me it's a place you go to find what's in your own mind. Consciousness raising, self-awareness, getting control of your own life. When you spoke to me about your experiences, they rang true. You'd probably get something out of studying karate yourself."

"Maybe, but I still prefer to do all my therapy lying down."

Hyams smiles, and for the first time it seems genuine.

"You know," he says, "when I first got out here and started covering the business, I used to resent people like you."

"And what did I ever do to you?"

"Nothing, which is my point. I just resented the success of people like you, no matter what it took for you to get there. Rich, pampered, egotistical. But that was my own insecurity. When I did interviews back then, I used to get aggressive. I'd needle the person until I got a reaction. I'm sure many of them still resent that. But the funny thing with all this is that in the interview we did, I was actually listening. I was hearing someone talk about a path they found that wasn't all that different from my own."

The Acrobat feels so naked in the moment that he knows the Treatment is far from complete. In a way that feels reassuring.

"Joe, my understanding from my lawyer Stanley is that you have a proposal on how to settle this whole thing. I'm quite eager to hear it."

"It's simple, really. I write your story. Your whole story. You get to share your life with an eager public, and I write it for publication. You are the king and I am back in the king's good graces. The mess goes away. Even though this mess is completely your own doing."

"Your tact is breathtaking, Joe."

"Hey, I listened to you, and I wrote exactly what you told me. And frankly, it was one of the few times I've heard a Hollywood star actually say something at all genuine."

"Yes, we're encouraged to avoid that sort of thing at all costs."

"So are you glad you said it, or are you not?"

"I think I probably am."

"Then there it is."

"Well, maybe I will tell my whole sorry story, then. And you'll make some money out of it as well."

"That's the plan. Your lawyer proposed I get all the proceeds."

"Did he, now? That sounds suspiciously like something *your* lawyer would say."

"Oh, no, my lawyer said winning a judgment of a half million dollars was going to be a breeze, given the tape recordings and photographs and my documents confirming the whole interview. This plan allows me to make the money, and all it costs you is some of your time."

"I suppose that makes some sense."

"But your lawyer also told my lawyer it might be a good idea if I use some of that money to buy you something nice. Like a Rolls-Royce."

"Well, it's the thought that counts!"

"Tribute for the king, if you will."

"Yes, tribute for the king, indeed."

Hyams stands up from the couch and extends his hand. "All is well in the kingdom, then?"

"All is never truly well in the kingdom," the Acrobat says, shaking the hand extended to him.

1945

AFTER THE PAPERS HAD been drawn up, and the court had been quietly petitioned to finalize the decree, the Acrobat and the Heir sat on the sofa for one last chat as spouses. It seemed, to him, the right thing to do.

Charles the butler was, as always, hovering in the back. Charles was, in truth, Barbara's only dependable man, ready with her drink, the two of them as oddly allied as her Coca-Cola and vodka. The Acrobat sufficed with a Gibson that he only sipped the top off and then put aside.

They talked a while about her son, Lance, who was now nine years old and a perfectly good boy, attended to by his governess.

"He's so quiet you hardly know he's around," the Acrobat said.

"He's away at boarding school, darling."

"My, is it just you and me here, finally, and now that it's all over?"

"Charles is standing right there, darling."

"Charles is family, dear! I'm speaking of your various hangers-on."

"I gave them the night off."

"So that we might comb through the rubble of all this? How generous of them."

"How did we fail? Marriage seemed like such a wonderful idea at the time."

"I'd say we both have some work to do, don't we?"

"What did you expect was going to happen?"

"I thought we'd change each other for the better."

"Why would you possibly have thought that?"

"Because that's the way it happens in my movies."

"You wanted to live nattily ever after . . ."

"I always do. It's in the script!"

"So you'll have another script now, darling. And what will the plot be?"

"How do you mean?"

"What kind of woman did you really want?"

"Someone just like you, except for the difficult parts."

"I could say the same. We never talked about children. Did you want one?"

"We never got that far, did we? I worried you'd think it was a way of my getting the hooks into you."

"Well, you're the first husband I ever had who refused my money."

"I'm doing perfectly all right on my own."

"I'd say you're doing quite well. It was only being with me that could make you look like a money-grubber, which of course it has."

"Yes, I suppose I'll live with that. What do we look for after this? And what kind of man will you end up with?"

"Someone without stilts, I suppose. And you?"

"Someone who owns one or fewer castles."

"Where else am I going to put my money? You can only have so much jewelry."

"But you do have so much jewelry."

"Makes me happy."

"I'll concede that castles and gems are a better investment than the sheiks and earls who are always underfoot around here."

"Oh, you hated them a bit too much. They're harmless."

"Titled nobility are never harmless, dear."

"You just hate them because they didn't earn their way in life. But I didn't, either, did I? And I didn't choose it, either, did I?"

"You make great wealth sound like an absolute affliction."

"But it is, in a way, isn't it?"

"Well, you seem to make the most of it."

"Don't be cruel, now."

"I'm sorry."

"So put on your list not to marry an heiress. Let her earn her keep, by God!"

"I'll keep that in mind."

"And maybe someone who drinks less? I know that has always bothered you."

"I used to think I drank too much. Then you came into my life."

"It's a hazard of the life, you know that, darling. Just as being so charming goes with the life you chose."

"Is that my affliction, then?"

"If that's how you like to think of it, certainly."

"But, Barbara my dear, I really wish you'd think about drinking less vodka. For your own good."

"I quite frequently think about drinking less vodka.

Sometimes I switch to gin."

"Yes, there it is."

"Well, you're rid of me now. Why worry about it?"

"Because I actually care about you. You must realize that."

"That's sweet. But I don't think anyone really cares about me. I don't think I deserve it. That's why I have to fill the place up with princes and duchesses."

"And earls and sheiks."

"I don't even really like them."

"You know that I don't."

"But we dislike them for different reasons, don't you see? I dislike them because I recognize them for exactly what they are. You don't like them because you worry you're getting to be very much like them."

"That's a shocking thing to say!"

"But you didn't say I wasn't right."

"I think you've been drinking too much just now."

"I do my best thinking when I've been drinking too much. You're just shocked because I've gotten to know you more than you thought."

"I wanted to find a woman who I knew didn't need anything from me."

"But you didn't realize I needed everything from you, except for the money."

1959

MIDSUMMER. PAST THE CRISIS. *Northwest* has come out, and he is not ruined after all. But he somehow comes out of it still feeling aggrieved.

The premiere was in Chicago, the midpoint of the film's

journey. He stayed home. He'd had an awful time in the making of the picture. He and Hitch had parted with tensions between them. Halfway through the shooting of the film, the Acrobat had been exhausted and doubtful. Every scene but one centered on his character, Roger O. Thornhill. He could feel the pressure of it being "his" film to botch. The script seemed constantly in rewrite, and the scenes made no sense to him. After a particularly difficult stretch, he'd begun to rebel. But in his deference to Hitch, he argued instead with the screenwriter, Lehman.

"I can't make heads or tails out of this," he'd said to the writer, who usually sat at the edge of the set, looking pale. Lehman had the unenviable task of taking Hitch's fragmented ideas and turning them into a story.

"It will all make sense in the end," Lehman said, rather unconvincingly.

"You've written me a David Niven script, and it's lousy on top of that."

"Actually, I wrote it with James Stewart in mind."

"Well, I don't understand what any of this has to do with Mount Rushmore, either."

"Hitch says people will remember it," Lehman said, evenly.

"And why don't we know what's on the damned microfilm?"

"That's just the MacGuffin, as Hitch says."

"This picture is going to be a disaster for me," the Acrobat finally said to Hitch later that day. "It's a terrible script and I desperately want out of this picture! Most of my pay is going to the Internal Revenue Service as it is!"

"Much too late for that," Hitch said.

They hadn't talked much from then on. But the Acrobat went on trouping, as Pender taught him, trying to squeeze out whatever he could in what he had already dismissed as a career low point.

And this was another picture in which he worried he was too old (or at least far older than the character he played, per the original script). Nowhere was this more apparent than the fact that the woman playing his mother was only eight years older than him. And Jessie Landis didn't let him forget it.

"I conceived him when I was seven," she'd kept saying on the set, to many laughs but for his own. Four years earlier, in *To Catch a Thief*, Jessie played the mother of a much-younger woman, with the presumption being that their respective characters were near-contemporaries. Now, like many an older actress, she was made the aged mother of a man trying to remain young.

Jessie needed to change to get more jobs. In the same way, the Acrobat had quietly recast himself, after his brief retirement in 1952. He was off the screen for such a short time, people seemed not to realize he'd retired at all. But what he had retired was the clown.

The clown had served him very well. And as a younger man, he'd enjoyed it thoroughly. Always willing to do what they asked, wear what they said to wear, and spout the lines they'd typed out for him. But in the films since his reemergence (*Thief* and *Affair* and *Indiscreet* and *Houseboat*), he presented as a more reserved man, a matured man, and no longer someone singing for his supper. He didn't so much announce this as simply reject any scripts that called on his now-retired comic self. Culling the pile was important, as was throwing in with directors who didn't want acrobatics. Not that he didn't dance once in a while; this was now selective. So subtle a change as to be largely unnoticed, but profound to him. He was regarding the world with a bemusement he'd previously found hard to hold. Roger Thornhill was a profoundly different man that he would have been before the hiatus.

Then the reviews began to come out. Hitch was praised as a genius; the Acrobat was mentioned as someone simply taking on the easy task of playing himself. *He's never been more at home,* was what the *New York Times* wrote. The Acrobat, reading the newspaper at breakfast after it had been flown in to Los Angeles overnight, tossed it aside in disgust.

Same old, same old, in other words. A man without need for dimension. A sleepwalker in his own pictures. A man who just had to "play himself" to succeed. Maddening, maddening, maddening.

Once one of his pictures has premiered, he regards it as dead and buried. He won't watch. What audiences see as reality he can only see as the reality behind it: the tense sets, the forests of equipment, the pressure of getting the scene right. In New York, where they'd gone to shoot the exterior scenes in Manhattan, he stayed burrowed in his regular suite at the Plaza until called down to do his business. When he returned to Los Angeles and they began to shoot the interiors, he felt a strange vertigo. Of seeing the exact replica of the Oak Room, a simulacrum with none of the substance, just weightless veneers hammered onto soft wooden scaffolds. Or the set for the room at the Plaza. He walked into a precise replica of the suite in which he'd stayed in New York. In the closet were the suits that belonged to George Kaplan, the nonexistent man his character was being mistaken for, after the United States Intelligence Service had invented the persona of Kaplan to flush out the spies. The suits looked like his own but proved an ill fit when he held one up; the Acrobat was a man behind a made-up name playing a man searching for a man who only existed as a made-up name, but whose suits seemed to confirm his existence. A literal clothes-make-the-man moment.

1952

LAX TO IDLEWILD FIRST, with a few days in New York City to grant selected audiences and rest a bit. Then BOAC, riding first class in a new de Havilland Comet 4 jetliner into London. Eight hours of flight instead of four days on a ship. At Heathrow, the car was waiting at the terminal and heads all around him turned: *Is that really him?* The slow crawl out of the exurbs; two slogging hours west with growing anxiety, pinned to the leather seat of the Rolls with the discomfort of a caged budgie. Then to the little house, greeted by the people he paid to look after her. Then through the door, and then facing her.

"Why, hello, love!" he said, flashing his famous smile.

The old lady looked up at him as if not quite sure she wanted to be happy.

"Oh, hallo," she said.

He had the wrapped gift and he held it toward her; she motioned for him to put it on her dresser. She had the mien of someone imprisoned, though she'd endlessly refused to move from this place, her home now for so many years. Admittedly, when she had refused his offer to move her to Los Angeles, he'd felt a gale of relief.

"I'm surprised to see you here," she said. "Always so busy, you."

"It's a busy life, Mother dear," he said back, as if reading a line from a script.

Bristol wasn't exactly Hollywood's antipode, but whenever he made the long journey there, he could only ponder how irreconcilable these two places were.

Bristol, a town of rain and grayness, from which he had fled to the inextinguishable California sun. Bristol, a tangled weave of medieval lanes, curving and turning back on themselves and dead-ending; Hollywood's orderly grids and wide sun-blanched freeways. Bristol, a place of complicated return; Hollywood, a place of complicated escape.

England always made him gloomy. He'd had every reason to let it, but he also acknowledged it had formed him, and who he was. He grew up in those soggy Bristol winters, and that barely heated home, after his mother had gone. Roaming the rainy streets, then stumbling into the theater, with its blinding light and its chamber of heat, and the roaring laughter that killed the doleful silence he had come to know. He would be ever thankful he found it.

Now he was back, ensconced not in the old haunts but in a country manor, lent by the friends of important friends. Out the window, rain whipped across gray fields from gray skies, and even with a fire in the hearth the Acrobat felt bereft.

He was always that way after visits to his mother. He'd entered her small home filled with cheer, but her brittle affect was more than just British; it was more than just age. And it brought him down. He sat and smiled and held her hands and asked after her health; she could not emerge quite enough from herself to meet him halfway. Whatever troubled her those years ago, when she went away, had never fully abated. She was seventy-five now, set in her small ways and always just distant enough for him to feel an ache. But the visit was done, and he and Betsy were staying on for a bit.

In his bedroom now, listening to the rain, he was thinking of ending things. But he wasn't sure exactly what to end. Or how. What he knew was that he was desperately unhappy and he didn't know how to cure it. Ending marriages had turned out to be a wholly ineffective tactic. It went beyond that. It was about him. Maybe he was never truly as happy as he'd briefly been at the Empire, when it had been such a bright cure for such a dark time of his life. He came to realize, so many years later, that all of them—old Melvyn, the stagehands and actors and hangers-on, and later Pender—knew what they'd been doing. They were giving a sad boy with a sad life a chance to be part of something that, while not family, felt very much like family. He moved through all that while childishly oblivious to it; he never thanked anybody or expressed the kind of love he had since realized he held for them. The person he had become, he was coming to despise. Not for any reason other than that it just wasn't the answer.

He and Betsy, in the spirit of their accommodations, were served formal dinners. Back in Los Angeles, they might have eaten with trays in front of the television. But their British hosts, themselves off to warmer climes, had left staff instructions for the full royal treatment.

They duly complied. He in black tie and she in a gown, sitting at the long table as the butler directed the meal with a series of nods and gestures as the servers ghosted in and out.

"I feel as if I'm trapped in one of my own films," he said to Betsy.

She laughed, but then he said, "I actually mean that, dear."

And she saw the look on his face.

"Are you quite all right?"

"Tired, I suppose."

"And is that all?"

"Not completely."

"Well, tell me then."

He glanced at the stony butler, at attention at the edges. Betsy laid down her utensils and rose from her distant chair. As the butler lurched forward to help her, she waved him off. She dragged the chair along the parqueted floor to the place close by the Acrobat, and said in a softer voice, "But are you quite all right?"

"I'd truthfully say possibly, and possibly not."

Betsy turned to the butler and said, "May we be left alone for a few moments?"

The butler silently retreated.

"Butlers are trained to not listen to private conversations," the Acrobat said.

"Oh, I'm quite sure. But tell me now."

"I've reached a bad patch. I just don't want to keep on with how things are."

She was quiet for a moment, then said, "Are you talking about our marriage?"

"Oh, no! I'm talking about my own sorry state. And I need you to help me."

"What's going on, dear?"

"I feel in an empty way. After all this, I feel more misery than when I was a penniless boy. More miserable than when I had to scrape for every chance and wondered what would become of me. It was the aspiration that chased away the fear that I was nothing at all."

"You know I know how that is," she said.

"Yes, indeed I do."

"How bad is it?"

"Quite bad."

"Such as, hard to get out of bed in the morning?"

"Past that, really."

"Oh, dear. How far past?"

"Even difficult to pull a tuxedo on."

"I'm alarmed. Tell me more."

"I need to put an end to the man I have become, by whatever means."

"You don't mean ... well, *you know*."

"No, not *you know*. But something much like it. The problem is, I don't know who I am if I'm not that man."

"Well, you're Archie, dear."

"Archie may be as dead and buried as his poor brother John. And I suppose this 'Grant' fellow has slowly and willfully smothered him."

"Oh, I think Archie's under there somewhere."

"He would have been someone else, and I'm not sure that would have gone so well, either. Being that fellow—or at least that sort of fellow—did my father in, didn't it?"

"But you transformed. And so you can transform again. Take it on, dear. Be a third man."

"The Third Man? I turned that role down years ago. Orson Welles, remember?"

"Well, I'm glad to know you can be clever and sound suicidal at the same time."

The butler was hovering on the threshold and Betsy took notice. "Just a bit more, please," she said.

The butler receded.

"A third man," the Acrobat said. "What would his name be?"

"What does it matter? Does he even need a different name, if *you* know who he is?"

"But I feel as if the man we know as Cary needs to expire. His best days are behind him. At least he'll be remembered for *None but the Lonely Heart*. And maybe for a few other trifles. And that's something, isn't it?"

"There never really was a man named Cary, dear. He was concocted by the studio. The question is, who is the man pretending to be him?"

In bed that night, he summoned no sleep. That was largely the case in England, where he often imagined what he'd be doing in Los Angeles, where he and Betsy would be having a cocktail and getting ready for dinner. She was someone he loved; he wondered how she could love him back, a man within a man within a man.

The man in front of the camera did those things the role expected of him, and that the role allowed him: He romanced his leading ladies almost reflexively. He charmed the masses. He struggled with the things that his life as Archie put on him: He couldn't seem to charm his own mother, whose love of him he frequently doubted; he endlessly sought proxies for his distant father and illusory older brother. He wanted a family while he was equally terrified of having it. He wondered if he'd be any good at all as a parent.

But here was Betsy, standing with him.

He'd first seen her on a stage in London when he was back for the obligatory visits; on the way home, on the *Queen Mary*, this same woman had bumped into him in a ship's corridor two hours out to sea. He'd been on his way to have lunch with Elizabeth Taylor. Betsy had looked tired. She'd had a toothache.

When they got to talk, first at sea and then more formally after that on land, she'd poured out her own revelations: the once-wealthy family broken by the Great Crash in 1929; the usual patrician array of drinking and abuse and dishonesty. The solace of the show. He and she were alternate versions of each other, in some ways, and that in itself was braided with comfort and repulsion.

In the morning, at the long table, having hardly slept, he got right to it. The butler was hovering, but the Acrobat was past caring. He wanted to pack up and go home and be done with the worries.

Betsy was quiet, because she clearly knew the depth of his ruminations.

"I think I've made a decision on how to liquidate our unfortunate friend Cary."

Betsy looked at him closely, then said, "Do tell."

"I've decided he's retiring. I'll hang him up in the closet like a suit I don't care to wear anymore."

"Something that's gone out of fashion."

"To mothballs and cold storage. He can remain on film, never to be resurrected. But I, as a person, will be off the screen."

"Are you sure that's the answer? You're still young. Forty-eight is really quite young."

"I'd prefer to choose my exit before they throw me out the door."

"How is that?"

"This new way of doing things. The wild young actors, the directors who think they're the stars, and *television*, and all this other nonsense."

"And what might you do in your retirement, dear?"

"I'd do what any decent person does. I'd disappear."

The rain drummed on, and the winds rose. Betsy had gone off to nap. The Acrobat, in his own room, found the telephone and made the call to Los Angeles. It was three in the morning back there. He knew one person who would answer a phone. Far through the transatlantic static, through the clicking of station to station and then through wires strung across the broad continent, the sound of a phone being uncradled.

"This is Hughes . . ."

"Howard, it's me."

Hughes's voice was reedy through the line, and they both were practiced enough to silently count to three as their signals vaulted back and forth across a third of a planet.

"You knew I'd be awake," Howard said.

"Indeed I did. It's raining here in England, if you can believe that!"

"And this may surprise you, but it's not raining here in California."

"Well, Howard, here's the thing. I've decided to retire."

"Do you want me to talk you out of it?"

"No."

"Good. Because I find receding to be necessary. Then is there a reason why you called?"

"No, not exactly. Maybe I just wanted to hear a friendly voice. But, besides that, I'm reading the newspapers here and wondering why you're getting so involved in politics."

"How do you mean?"

"All the nonsense with this Senator McCarthy. You seem much too occupied with this communism talk. Are you all right?"

"Of course I'm all right. I'm damned concerned."

"I don't ever remember you paying much attention to politics. I don't even know how you vote."

"I've never voted in my life."

"So why this?"

"Well, friend, have you seen what Stalin has done under the flag of communism? Do you think we need these types in Hollywood?"

"They're just hobbyists, Howard. They're not real communists."

"They say they are!"

"It was just the fashion at one time. The opposite of the Nazis, and so forth. Our Jewish friends in particular saw that as fair play."

"They're still communists. And they won't be using my studio to sell their subversive wares, friend."

"But why do this to Charlie Chaplin?"

"Ah, there it is," Hughes said. "That's why you're calling me?"

"Let him have his moment. He's just premiered *Limelight* in London, and it's quite a celebration from what I'm reading. Now I'm hearing they might not even want to let him reenter the United States."

"Friend, the British may be soft on communism, but we're not. If I have my way, that picture will never be shown in America."

"But Charlie has never really done anything but make his pictures."

"He's a rabble-rouser."

"The man's an artist."

"He transmits dangerous messages."

"Howard, really now, how far will all this go?"

"Why, are you a communist, too?"

"Be serious. You know I'm a registered Republican."

"Oh, come off it. That's about your income taxes, we both know it."

"I'm not a communist, Howard. But I still do wonder how far this goes."

"It goes until we root out all the subversives."

"Howard, if you starting turning over all the rocks, you never know what you'll find."

"Then we had all better watch our rocks, friend."

Far Shore

HE CAN HEAR THE *pounding of the waves from a great distance, and there is that sudden sense of salt in the air he didn't have just a few steps back. He follows her, with her big bag slung on her shoulder, and her shoes in her hand as she walks barefoot on the sand.*

Along the beachfront, the boardwalk is filled with people. Out on the long pier, women in their white summer dresses and men in their linen suits stroll languorously, and gaze across the distances, and feel the ocean breeze. It's a world of candy-striped beach chairs and the whitecaps on the Channel and the kiss of late-summer sunshine.

"Do you want a treat, Archie?" she says, but she doesn't need him to answer. They climb the stone steps onto the promenade, where a man has a pushcart of flavored ices. The vendor lifts a red scoop into a paper funnel and hands it to Arch.

"But save room for dinner," she says with a smile.

They've been gone for months, after she told her husband she

*was going to the seaside to find some happiness. Father had grown
cross when Mother insisted that Archie should go with her, and on
the train, after it had pulled out of the station, he had felt a guilty
exhilaration. Father, clad in his dour mien. Mother, suddenly sunny
in this new journey, smiling as she had not in that blunt past life,
and telling Arch how much better yet their lives will become. Out the
train's window, the sky blew on and the clouds broke and dissipated.*

*They walk on the promenade now, no hurry and no sense of
worry or weight. She takes his hand and the warmth envelops him.
They'll watch the sun set from the window of their small room in
a clean place, simple and all they really need. Just life as it should
be, as it should have always been, as it would go on now. She'll put
him to bed and in those moments before sleep he'll think again of his
father and wonder if he's sad, or whether he truly cares that his son
is now gone from him.*

1959

AUTUMN. THE MONTHS DWINDLE toward a new decade, but in
Hollywood the weather is just as always, and hard to mark time
by. *Look* magazine approached him for an interview, and he'd
agreed. The LSD is part of his story now. To be that much more
up front about it is to defuse any notion, after Hyams's *Herald
Tribune* article, that he has anything at all to hide. The reporter,
named Laura Bergquist, first showed up and interviewed him
over several sessions during the filming of *Northwest*. But after
the Hyams article, she'd come back needing more on that area of
discussion. He shared his story now without compunction.

Why should I feel shame?

I'm finding a way to be a better person.

Happiness is possible, at any time of your life.

He offered what he could in the most honest way he could. He gave Dr. Hartman his blessing to speak about the Treatment. And he was open about his struggles with women and how that related to his mother's disappearance.

In the end, one line of the article has kept returning to mind, though.

There are Hollywood skeptics who wonder if the "new" Grant may not be the best character part he has ever played.

The phone rings one early-September night and the woman's voice is that of a stranger, but oddly familiar.

"It's Esther Williams," she says. "How are things?"

"Going swimmingly, I'd say."

She is silent, briefly, then says, "I'd like to talk to you about LSD."

He's only met her a few times. Knows her not at all, other than her aquatic films. It seems he can only picture her in her natural habitat. It elicits a momentary shudder about his own swimsuit scene in *Thief*, something he's always felt deeply embarrassed by.

"I read the article in *Look*," she says.

"Do tell. Well, I suppose *Look* magazine does get one some attention."

"Everyone's talking about it. About what you said. About your treatment."

"I suppose if I've become a product spokesman, I should be paid for it."

"I need to know what you know," she says. "I need to ease the pain."

"I never took you to be in pain."

"Nor did I of you. Funny how that is."

He realizes how hard that is to imagine, given her place

in those aqueous extravaganzas, confections that are as hallucinatory as some of his treatments. Technicolor has a way of making experiences feel saturated with feeling in a way that isn't true, even on the klieg-lighted sets.

"Esther, my advice to you is that if you do it, do so without fanfare. I can speak well of the experience, but maybe I shouldn't have done so publicly."

"Ron and Nancy Reagan say they're worried about you," Esther says. "But I want to know more."

"Well, bless their hearts. People shouldn't worry."

"Believe me, plenty are worried about you. But I know I need some way of coming out of this."

"Esther, let's have lunch sometime, then."

"Let's, indeed," she says. "Tomorrow?"

"How did you come across this phone number, Esther? Most people don't even know I have it."

"Betsy passed it on. She said you wouldn't mind."

Betsy was supposed to have been the last and lasting wife. She was supposed to have been the real-life Happily Ever After, the glowing *The End* when the music comes up and the screen goes to black and a future is certain. He knows that his audiences believe in that, the finality of outcomes, their inevitability. Roger O. Thornhill believes in marriage so much he takes it on for the third time just before credits roll, and audiences leave the theater warmed to the notion that all is to be well this time. Why should anyone be so sure?

Sometimes the Acrobat thinks of his various alter egos and their fates after the final credits. He imagines Nickie Ferrante of *Affair*, sitting with a scotch on the rocks as Terry, in her wheelchair now, packs the last of her things, the rest forwarded to her new apartment.

"But the Empire State Building, New Year's Eve," Nickie says.
"People change," Terry says quietly. "People grow. The Empire State Building idea was what left me this way. How could you even bring that up?" An affair to remember, now remembered differently.

John Robie of *Thief* only lasts so long before he's standing back on the terrace of his villa, phone to his ear. He's listening to Frances tell him, from her suite at the Carlton over in Nice, that the age difference was always a problem. She's heading back to America. She can't see being married to a convicted felon, an aging one at that, even if she'd been the one to set out to catch him. His criminal record makes it unlikely he'd get a visa, even if she did invite him to join her.

And Philip Adams and Anna Kalman, having been *Indiscreet*, can't overcome the wedge of him initially lying to her about his marital status. It's turned out to be a bigger issue than they imagined in their attraction. She's realized that the intensity of their flirtation never could fully patch the damage.

"You put me through hell with your lies, and like a fool I let you," Anna says.

The Acrobat can only see those outcomes, even as he wishes for an Ever After that's befitting one of his pictures. He wants his own Hollywood ending, but the problem is he actually lives in Hollywood. He *is* Hollywood, on some level, as is Betsy: driven by their ambitions and insecurities, maybe; trying to bond with other damaged souls. There are still those fans who tell him, as they accost him in his rare public forays, that his stories in some ways informed their own happy romances. It's the wood he carries, in service to other people.

In a particular session of the Treatment on a particular Saturday, he finds himself on a journey of the mind to a newly disturbing place. Afterward, he slowly relates these visions to Dr. Hartman: of hiding in a locked office, terrified as they come for him. In this office, he hears the approaching footsteps, and voices angry as they kick down other doors trying to flush him out. He's crawled behind a chair, more certain that when they find him, they will kill him.

"Do you know who they are?" Dr. Hartman says.

"Yes."

"And who are they, then?"

"My characters."

"Again?"

"Every character I ever played, together like a wild unhinged mob, coming to do me in. I always controlled them, but now they've broken free and they want to destroy me. Look at me. I'm still shaking."

"Hmm," Dr. Hartman says.

"So what do you think Dr. Freud would have made of that?"

"I think Dr. Freud might have needed a good stiff drink."

"I'd be doing the buying."

The doctor considers this vision further.

"But even we who are not actors play many roles, don't we?"

"I suppose."

"I play the doctor, the husband, the father, the son, the neighbor. Do I not create many characters?"

"But there was one especially disturbing part."

"Go on."

"Cary was outside that door. And Archie was, too."

"Then who was the you that was hiding from them?"

"I really have no idea."

The doctor is silent for a bit, then speaks.

"Have you ever felt ashamed of yourself?"

"I've been ashamed all my life."

"Do you believe that's justified?"

"I've never had the luxury of giving it much thought."

"But why?"

"Why not?"

"That's just being glib. I'd prefer a more satisfying answer."

"I certainly wish I had a better one."

"Are you ashamed of your true self, or afraid of being shamed for it?"

"Are those not one and the same?"

"Not at all."

"I'd love to be my true self, but what if the gossip magazines were to get wind of it?"

"I'm sure it's not as bad as all that!"

"I never thought it was bad at all. I try to offer love and respect and happiness, but I always have to look over my shoulder when I'm doing it."

He listens to the distant peal of a telephone ringing on a wire at the other end of the continent. It's late back there, but show people don't know how to live otherwise. The click of a phone being uncradled, and then that honeyed voice: "Yes?"

"Greta, it's me," he says.

"You? Who is 'me'?"

"You don't recognize my voice, Greta?"

"What I hear is someone doing a bad impression of my good friend. Are you a reporter, then?"

He laughs out loud.

"Yes, I always do a bad impression of that fellow. Can I tell you something personal that only you and I know?"

"Yes," comes the hesitant voice.

"When you came to visit at Santa Monica, with Noel, and the run in your stocking . . ."

Now it is she who bursts into laughter.

"I didn't think anybody noticed that!" she says.

"Everyone noticed that, dear."

"You're really starting to sound like a parody of yourself."

"I must be watching too many of my own movies," he says. "I just can't take my eyes off myself."

"Achh. I don't believe that for a second."

"Well, I suppose this is what I've let myself turn into."

"Everybody does that in their own way. But, is everything all right?"

"Smashing," he says.

"Enough to pick up the phone late at night?"

"Here's the thing. I've been thinking about going away, the way you've gone away. Hidden in plain sight."

"It's not so easy. You spend so long seeking the attention that you can't imagine you then have to fight it off. I thought everyone would just stop caring. The more I seek solitude, the more it's under assault."

"Our greatest fear becoming our greatest need."

"But you? Really? I had gotten to a point where I loathed showing up. The pictures made me so unhappy. You seem to be thriving."

"What gave you that impression?"

"Seeing your movies, of course."

"I feel I've done all I want to do," he says. "I've made my money. I want there to be something else ahead of me. I tried retiring once before, but I failed. I want to do it right when I try again."

"It's nice to think there's a future. I spend a lot of time in the past, when I'm alone, and when I'm feeling blue."

"The old days. You know who I ran into today? Jack Kelly."

"That explains the call, then. That old gang on the way up."

"And all the others who fell by the wayside."

"I wonder if they worry about it as much as we do," she says. "I'd guess they moved on to happy lives."

"You're not happy?"

"Depends on the time of day. But it isn't as important as I thought it would be. It brought me enough money to live in style. But you? Do you really think you'd like obscurity?"

"I've been experimenting with it."

"Well, let me give you some advice. If I had to do it all over again, I wouldn't have been so fast trying to shut the door behind me. Let them see you once in a while. Let them take a few pictures. Show up here and there. The only thing that keeps them interested in me anymore is their fascination with my effort at complete invisibility. I set up the trap on myself. I'm the Loch Ness monster instead of just being quietly retired . . ."

They say their goodbyes, and when he hangs up, it's still a breezy California night with a bit of light still on the horizon. Greta's been gone so long from the scene it's felt a bit like a séance; if she were more joyful about escaping all this, it would have been more instructive. He knows he's begun the next step, no matter how long it's going to take.

1954

A WEARY TRAVELLER, WALKING on rain-lashed streets of a town he no longer truly knew. A pilgrim, back to face spirits and portents. As often as he returned here, he ventured rarely; when he came here he mostly moved alone, as he did now in the steady sheets of raindrops, undisguised but with one hand holding a cinched collar against the weather and with the other hand tugging the brim of a hat so that others passing by, under their umbrellas, would make no note of him. A Sunday night, and in Bristol City Centre there were few people about anyway, and he'd walked from his hotel room at the Royal, and past the worried-looking doormen, and plunged down the narrow side streets of his memory.

It wasn't so easy to get lost, as much as he might have wanted to. Everything in this city seemed to oddly circle back on itself. Outside the Royal, outside that tight compartment he so often limited himself to, he wanted to see what was left of what he knew, so long ago.

He found his way to the old Empire, not what it once was, not in a long time: first a movie theater, quite naturally, and now perhaps as naturally a BBC facility. Television, the rampaging beast, devouring all that was holy. But they'd thought the same thing when the cinema devoured all in its way.

The streets were slickened with rain and light, the reflections like rough brushstrokes on a dark canvas. At a portal that was once that old stage door, Melvyn's ghost must still have roamed about: long dead, long forgotten, but remembered brightly in the Acrobat's own mind. Melvyn, a man about whose demise little was likely found, if one were to search. A tidy grave perhaps, with a flat stone, maybe made possible by a bit of money from a hat passed around the old theater. A plot, perhaps, among the tilted crosses of Holy Souls or Ridgeway Park; Melvyn had never once held forth on matters of religion. As old as he'd been, his passing could not have been so long after he'd sat in the dressing room with the Great Devant and a boy who wanted greatness for himself; the Acrobat regretted all the people whom he never bothered to keep up with or to honor, as he rushed toward his own destiny.

The hour was late; he walked on. The clock's midnight chime from Great George, the mighty bell of the university tower. It must have been cocktail hour in Los Angeles with the sun in the orange blossoms, but he was on the other side of the world, upside-down at least in spirit.

Not far from the hotel, where the small boats rocked in the undulant waves of the harbor inlets, he stood before the Hippodrome, its blocky façade reminiscent of a house of worship. Indeed, the theater revealed as much about the human soul as any church; sin and redemption and honor nightly graced its boards. But this place was different as well. The fire of 1948 had gutted it. Now rebuilt, it was a place he could enter but not truly return himself into. He stood at its front for a while, then walked back to the hotel in the rain.

He hadn't been to the West Country much, and certainly not to Bournemouth since the old troupe days before America. Now on this gray Monday morning he'd hired a car. He chose not the usual Rolls but rather a hackney, in this case an only moderately comfortable Beardmore, with a driver who seemed less interested in talking than he was. The ride was two hours, with a long stretch of the A350 that passed fog-shrouded barley fields. In places, withering lavender sat in endless rows, the blooms gone dull now and muted by the weather. The summer was at its end, with equinox just past. But only weeks before he'd been shooting on the Riviera, being driven by Grace in that 1953 Sunbeam Alpine two-seater, a gorgeous white-hot woman in a gorgeous silvered car with him along for the ride. They edged the cliffs overlooking Monaco as the second unit got the shot from above. Most of the close-up car scenes had been shot static on the soundstage in Los Angeles with backdrop footage. But sitting in that car looking down at Monaco, he'd felt a bit of a thief himself.

So, at the end of filming, he'd come to Bristol to do his requisite visits with his mother, who remained her steely and intractable self. Duties completed, and without the warmth he'd known on the set of this film. Jessie Landis, an old trouper herself now playing Grace's mother, was always up for some laughter. Something about the way old hands took to each other.

The complexities of visiting his actual mother always weighed heavily. She had her own troubles and there'd never be a major change there, no matter how much his father might have embellished things at that time. There was always that undercurrent, that abrasion, that callus hardened over whatever pains lay beneath. The Acrobat never spent much time thinking about his lost brother, tried purposely not to, but he suspected she thought about it all the time, that favorite son not easily replaced.

John, the ethereal brother, had shaped him as if standing over his shoulder, despite having died years before Baby Archie opened his eyes to the world and breathed his first. His mother's stifling attentions were, he began to realize much later, of a trauma. And Arch had lived the odd experience of being an only child who was yet second-best. She watched him play with cautions and prohibitions: *Don't do this* and *Don't do that,* to where he felt constricted in every direction and allowed to venture nothing. Then, as suddenly, she was off on extended holiday, leaving him to his own uncertain devices, warning him off nothing.

As a boy, he had visions of John as he would have been. He imagined the man who would have come out of a child who died so young, and one he never knew.

And, of course, this mythic John had looked nothing much like his parents, and much more like Arch's favorite movie stars. In those silent-movie days, John didn't talk much, letting his actions do the talking. The cowboy star Tom Mix often came to mind, though Arch wasn't partial to Westerns; it was just the confidence that oozed from the man. And in some strange way, he seemed to have looks that could qualify him as a Leach, without reducing him to actually being a Leach. Dark eyebrows, sharp face and strong neck, but without the monochromatic glumness Arch only knew of his parents. There was something easy and contained about Tom Mix's manner, so unlike the stage actors who had to shout and gesticulate to be understood up in the cheap seats. Arch imagined his dead brother like that, as an adult: man who knew himself.

For a while, he fantasized that Tom Mix actually was his brother. The math didn't prove out: John, had he lived, would have been eighteen when *The Heart of Texas Ryan* came to the local screen; Tom Mix was probably in his midthirties. But that didn't stop thirteen-year-old Arch from imagining that his brother not only had not died as a child, but had somehow been sent on "long holiday" and ended up on a blue-sky ranch in the American West, where he'd befriended all manner of man and beast, acquired an extraordinarily large cowboy hat, and wooed the girl, if not all of them. Arch fancied the idea of this. It was only walking home alone from the theater that he realized that in real life, his brother would surely have become one of the young men boarding the ships in the harbor, heading for a war where death seemed a distinct certainty.

When he visited his mother now, in her old age and his midlife, he wondered if she'd have been any better off if John had survived his childhood and then not survived the European trenches. Would Arch have even been born if not for his brother's death? The visits to his mother stirred these ramblings up for him, and as much as he was happy to see her, he was equally happy to have seen her.

* * *

239

But that was done. His mother had been attended to. There was always that moment when he went to kiss her cheek and she reflexively turned away; even as she approached eighty years of age in her strange afterlife, she could wound him. He sometimes loathed himself for being relieved when the visits were done.

But now he was in a cab on its way to Bournemouth, looking for another ghost. He'd hired a discreet investigator the last time he'd come to England; he'd gotten periodic updates since, addressed to Mr. A. A. Leach, by way of his studio office. Leach mail was to be left unopened by his secretaries.

Betsy didn't know about this excursion. She was back in Los Angeles after her time in Monaco with him; the marriage was not what either of them might have called perfect, but it was sustaining itself, despite him seeming to fall in love with every leading lady he worked with. So, on his own, and in England alone for the first time in a long while, today was the day for a long-planned, much-dreaded sortie.

At the edges of Bournemouth, tightly packed hedgerowed farmsteads gave way to tightly packed brick cottages, as the rain began to splatter the windscreen and the driver looked at his penciled directions laid across his lap. Down through, following the signs to Boscombe Pier, then looking for Lytton Road. Slowing, then slowing some more, then a small side street, then to a stop. A tidy little house in the row, as narrow as a slice of bread snug in its loaf.

"Here we are, then," the driver said, his first utterance since Bristol.

As long a drive as it had been, the Acrobat was still as yet unprepared. He had his raincoat across his lap, and as he got out of the car he pulled it over his shoulders and hurried to the front of the place. He came to the door and could smell in the air something cooking, spicy, maybe tarragon. Looking at his piece of paper, he knocked and heard stirring within. The door opened, and he was looking at a thin woman of roughly his own age, her hair cropped and tight, her face a bit drawn but unmistakably shocked. She just stared.

"Mrs. Charnley, I presume?"

She served the tea with her hands shaking enough to rattle the spoons on the saucers. She couldn't look him in the eye.

He'd announced, when she'd opened the door and gasped at the sight of him, that he was trying to figure out if her deceased husband had been an old friend of his.

"That hardly seems possible," she'd said, quite reflexively.

But here he was, sitting on a quilt-covered chair as she brought out the tea. He'd suggested he tell her the story, and she was not inclined to slam the door in his face. She knew who he was. Everybody knew who he was.

She seated herself on her sofa and poured the tea. The Acrobat was afire with the urge to plunge into all his questions, but he held on. Then she handed him his cup, and he nodded, and she said, flatly, "I cannot imagine how you would have known my Cecil."

That name was a surprise that had arrived with the investigator's letter: He'd only known him as Charnley, though Pender sometimes called him "Ace." Cecil Charnley, deceased 1952 here in Bournemouth, seemed the only person who, by age, could have matched the boy in his memory. But that was if he'd been born somewhere in the edges of London, if he'd been in the service, and if he'd fought in the war. The Acrobat knew none of these things for sure. He'd assumed all of it.

"Well," he said to the widow, "I don't know for a fact we did know each other, which is why I stopped by. I had to do it this way, I hope you understand. The press, and so forth."

She nodded. "Yes, the press rarely pays me mind," she said.

"But your husband did grow up in Brixton or thereabouts, didn't he?"

"Not quite. He grew up in Croydon. But his family came there from Bath."

"That's close enough. And well, he was an acrobat, in his younger days . . ."

She grinned broadly. "Oh, no, not my husband. He was never an acrobat."

"Did he have a brother who was, or a cousin?"

"He only had a sister. Cousins, he had, but I doubt. They were all lardy fellows. Can't see any acrobats there! Besides, they all lived up north, Leeds and around there."

"This was before the first war, I'm talking about. He would have been seventeen. I wonder of you might have some photos of him from back then."

Mrs. Charnley shook her head. "No photos I know of. He didn't talk much about anything before the war. He came home, got a job with the Royal Mail, and did that for thirty-one years. I met him in 1927, in our church. We had a quiet life."

"He was a postman?"

"Cecil? No, he was a sorter. Mostly he was a train sorter. We lived in Manchester for years. He'd board the mail train at Manchester London Road, and sort mail all the way to London, and then again all the way back out. Every day. They didn't even have a window to look out of. I bet he'd have liked to be a postman, to have been out of doors. But his leg . . ."

"What about his leg?"

"Well then, I'm certain you have the wrong man here. In the Argonne, he took the shrapnel and it damaged the nerves of his left leg. It was right at the very end, just a few days before the armistice. He had a terrible limp, and struggled all about with a cane. He put on weight, with the job he had, and he got a bit hunched."

"But then he might have been an acrobat. Before the war."

"Even still, I can hardly imagine Cecil as an acrobat. It's not conceivable. He'd never told me about any such thing."

He knew to back off a bit now.

"You see, I was in a troupe, as a boy, and there was a fellow named Charnley who went off to war. I'd just always wondered."

"Well there's his picture, just after we were married. That was 1929. As I say, we married a bit late."

"Children?"

"Of course, children. A boy and a girl."

The photo was framed in silver, atop a small end table. The Acrobat looked at it, a thick man with a cane and his hair slicked back from shining temples, seeming to be trying to muster a smile. The Acrobat had no idea. He was realizing that whatever image he'd retained in his head of Charnley might not have still been accurate. He'd attached the face to other faces so that they all ran together.

"This could well have been him," he said. "Possibly."

"You know, he was originally from up near Manchester. His father moved, looking for work. He was born in Bury. In fact, he used to say, 'I was born in Bury, and I'll be buried in Bourne.' We came down here on his pension and some savings. We thought about starting a little business, maybe an ice cream cart. He wasn't one to reminisce when life was all ahead of us. You know, he was a happy man, satisfied with life, even cheerful when he was dying."

"How did he pass?"

"Cancer of the lungs. Taken too young. But after the war, he always said every extra minute was a bonus."

"Did he know who I am?"

"Everyone knows who you are."

"And he didn't recognize me, from the old days? When you went to see my pictures?"

"We didn't go to many of your pictures, sorry to say."

"Really? Why not?"

"Cecil didn't think very much of you," she said. "As a *performer*. He said you were much too broad for his tastes. Too desperate, too loud, is what he said. Playing it too big, he said."

"He'd have made a very fine critic."

"He said he could see right through fellows like you. In truth, he said you were never very much his cup of tea."

1959

THE SET IS A PLACE of familiarity and of drudge. Shooting a few pickups and close-ups and piecing together patches on other location scenes. Like most films, this one is winding down and he'll be glad when it's done. He's already gotten the script for the new venture, his first film of the next decade. *The Grass Is Greener* will shoot in England, in April 1960. It will return him to familiar terrain, playing a shambled earl on an antiquated estate; he's to be reunited with a leading lady, Deborah, and a director, Stanley Donen, who will be as familiar as a pair of comfortable old slippers. He's ready to be done with the navy, even this comedic one. The picture is to be released in December, at Radio City, and he plans to be there: He owns a stake in the film, and money is money.

On the set, as usual, the first person he always sees is Scotty, the gaffer.

"Scotty, my dear boy, how are you?"

"Boss, I'm well."

"You look frightfully tense."

"Same old bullshit. I want a 5K key light and what do they do? Tell me a 4K is going to work just fine."

"I don't suppose you could just move it closer."

"You know better than that, Boss. It would pick up the oil in every pore on your face."

"We mustn't have that!"

"Damn right we mustn't. Don't think I don't know all your secrets by now."

"Scotty, I admire your persnickety nature."

"Is that a joke? Because none of this is funny. You all depend on me so you never have to think about it."

"Point taken, Scotty."

"Because I bet you never did."

"Did what?"

"Think about it."

"No, Scotty, that's where you're wrong. I can tell you what a well-known star of his day, maybe the greatest star of all, imparted to me."

"Wait, Boss—you took advice from an actor?"

"I did."

"I strongly advise against that."

"Does that mean you don't want to hear what he said?"

"Only if it will change my life."

The Acrobat regards Scotty's ravaged, pocked face, and says, "Unlikely."

He has found himself missing Betsy. They've been separated for more than a year, but he still calls her as if they are just away from each other on other pretenses. He hears rumors of her seeing other men, and who is he to object?

"Will you be with me again for Christmas this year?" he'd

said on his call the night before. He had to admit he was relieved when she'd picked up the phone.

"I haven't thought about Christmas," she said. "Won't you be in New York premiering the new picture?"

"I'll be back before the holiday. Won't you come over?"

"You hate to be alone and so do I," she said. "Should that be a reason for us to spend a holiday together?"

"It's as good as any."

"Well, maybe I will, then."

"I sometimes wonder why we're even apart."

"Do you, now?"

"I know I have a wandering nature."

"You're quite nomadic in matters of love, I'd say."

"I don't know why we can't accept love where we find it. Maybe I need it more than other people."

"What you want is to do what your heart desires. And do as you may. But I can't go back to that. I love you, dear, but it's better this way."

"I suppose."

"But I will look forward to Christmas, if you want me to."

"I do. I very much do."

"Well, let's confirm a few days before. It may be that your heart will desire to stay in New York, or fly off to Paris. And if you want to, you go right ahead."

Exiting the set, the Acrobat needs to move through the gantlet of extras, a couple of dozen from an adjacent production who have already been dismissed for the day but linger, to see the stars. He wades through, smiling and nodding. They've all been warned that they're not here as fans, but rather employees, but still they can hardly contain themselves. Yet they intuitively respect the fourth wall that cannot be broken without the prospect of termination. As he walks, he waits to see who's brave, or foolish enough. And what he sees ahead is a very pretty face. He waits that small beat before truly meeting her eyes, then says, "Did you enjoy your day?"

"I'm enjoying it right now . . ."

"Where are you from, my dear?"

"Davenport, Iowa. You've probably never heard of it."

"To the contrary. At one point in my career I was with a traveling troupe, and I certainly did a few tumbles in your very city. Once upon a time, and perhaps again in the future. But where do you make your home now?"

"I have an apartment in Echo Park that I share with two other girls."

"Ah, I'm in Beverly Hills."

"I believe that's a known fact."

"Care for a lift?"

"That's really not on your way."

"But not so far off it."

She's gotten in the Rolls feeling in control, and he'll slowly reverse that. She may presume why he invited her, but his motives are so much simpler right now. He just needs to see a fresh face with fresh dreams, to remind him.

They drive and he does as he always does, the gallant thing, taking an acute interest in her hopes and dreams though he knows these are really no different than countless other young actresses, and no different than his own tale: a pretty face, wanting to be noticed.

"I just always knew it would work out," she said. "In this picture I have a line, and on the next I'll have more lines, and then I'll land a real part," she says.

"That's certainly how it worked for me."

She'd been the prettiest girl in Davenport, no doubt; someone told her she had talent and she chose to overlook why someone might say that if it weren't true. She has that instilled confidence of someone who's never been unwelcome anywhere, but now she will test her limits in Hollywood, the toughest proving ground, where egos go to be crushed. She's testing her limits right now, he sees, and he's already going sour.

"Did I mention you're my mother's favorite movie star?" she says. "Mommy grew up with a crush on you, so I guess that runs in the family."

His smile is as forged as an iron mask, yet never unconvincing.

"How delightful to hear!"

"But my father always says you're overrated."

"Well, everyone knows that!"

She isn't getting the response she seems to want.

"Where are we dropping you, then?" he says.

"I thought you were luring me to your place . . ."

"No, I believe we're giving you a lift home. Echo Park, right?"

The driver, Albert, is looking at him through the rearview mirror, and in it the usual silent assent.

They drive into her neighborhood with the car attracting the usual attention. A man in his yard, watering his lawn with a hose, stares. A woman sitting on her front stoop stands to get a better look.

"It's as if these people have never seen a Rolls-Royce before," the Acrobat says.

"Well, you've been living in Beverly Hills a long time," she says.

But he's only deflecting, because what the sidewalk gapers are looking at is him. An old woman waves to him from a street corner as Albert pulls up to a stop sign; the Acrobat issues a rather papal wave back in the old woman's direction.

"It's like being with an emperor," the actress says, as he tries to recall her name, or if he heard it in the first place.

"All of life is a royal procession, if you let it be."

"My, isn't that a delightfully sunny outlook!"

"It's the only way I know how to be."

"Just like in the movies."

"Yes," the Acrobat says, nodding to Albert to get this girl out of the car. "Just like that."

The

A POOR MAN, WALKING *long straight roads. It's been an epic trek home. The edges of the city slowly become apparent; more cars, more buildings, fewer cabbage fields and citrus groves. Warrens of modest houses. Dry hour after dry hour he trudges on. His cheap clothing grates on his skin and the heat saps him. But he must get home. The journey seems endless.*

But he can anticipate the arrival. Back to accustomed pleasures. A bath, clean clothes, and a drink. Sit by the pool with a Gibson in his hand, perhaps. Eat a fine dinner with candles lighted.

His adventures among the populace have been a lark, something like a brief return to harder times. The long way back from there has been unexpected. There lies a chasm between these worlds. In the middle is just the endless repetition of the same gas stations, storefronts, and parking lots. The normal trappings of normal lives. Cars pass by but he seems the only one on foot, and he sees from those car windows the looks of deep suspicion toward himself, a man who lacks means and maybe self-respect. If they only knew. A Rolls-Royce is most often at his disposal. He doesn't know why he doesn't just call to have himself picked up; he hasn't seen a phone and has just pushed ever onward.

He finally reaches Sunset Boulevard, coming into West Hollywood, where the traffic gets heavier but it still seems as if he is the only person on foot. It's getting toward late afternoon. The sun is dropping steadily. He passes the Gaiety Diner, where through the window a waiter at the door watches him pass.

Then, farther on, an explosion of glass. He reflexively jerks his hands up to protect his face. He looks down and sees the brown shards of a beer bottle. Someone has thrown this at him, and just barely missed. He can hear the receding laughter. Up ahead, a battered, paint-peeled car speeds away with a young man hanging out of the passenger window, grinning manically.

He just wants to get home, which feels simultaneously close by and still so far to reach. He has come through Hollywood and is now on the quiet streets of Beverly Hills. He keeps his gaze on the sidewalk ahead of him, but a while later, he looks to see a Los Angeles police cruiser slowing as it passes, going the other way, the cop giving him a careful, sour look. But the cruiser doesn't stop, and he picks up his pace. As he walks on, he's more wary, ready to scramble behind a tree or fence to avoid being seen.

Finally, he is on his own street, as a stranger in a familiar land. Walls of high hedges stand endlessly on either side, meant to create privacy for the wealthy residents, but making a person on foot feel vulnerable and conspicuous. Looming ahead, finally, is his house, its rooftops high above the hedgerow.

He comes up the curving driveway, going through his pockets for a house key, but he has none. He reaches for the doorknob and realizes how filthy his hands have become. When he tries to push

the front door open, he finds that it's locked. He presses the doorbell
button, but no one answers. He presses again.

No one comes to greet him. He realizes his makeup may have
fooled them. He holds his sleeve against his face and rubs his cheek
against the coarse sleeve. But when he looks at the sleeve there isn't
makeup at all, only the stain of dust and sweat mixed into a grubby
sheen. He steps back onto the driveway.

Up in the second-floor window, a man is watching him. A man
who appears very much like someone he has played in a picture.
Tall, dark-haired, and dressed in a silk dressing gown. The man
looks down through the window for a bit, then turns away. And
then the drapes close.

Outside, it's getting dark. The house is unlighted other than that
window. The weather feels colder than it should be. He is heavy
with the fatigue of a very long journey from which he is not yet home,
despite being so close to it, always.

1958

HE WAS HIDING IN the bathroom. In his silk pajamas, and with
bare feet, having been too furious to even put on his slippers.
The Acrobat's marriage was dying and he didn't want to come
out of this small sanctuary. Betsy—his docile, aims-to-please,
adoring wife—had just told him to go fuck himself.

He held his ear to the door and couldn't hear a sound. The
funny thing was, she said it not with rage but with a sense of
tired dismissal. A sense of control. It was a side of her he'd never
seen, and he was horrified. She'd never uttered that word for
as long as he'd known her, and he'd leapt out of bed. He'd have
made a better choice to storm off to another part of the house.

She might have had good reason, though. The situation with

his co-star Sophia during the shooting in Spain of *The Pride and the Passion* was so obvious, he knew, that Betsy saw where it was all going. He just couldn't help himself. So Betsy decided to head back to America on an ocean liner. That seemed a rather pointed message. They'd met on an ocean liner, of course, and then he'd made a picture about love begun on an ocean liner. Now, for her solitary retreat, she went off on another ship: the *Andrea Doria*. How did anyone know the ship would sink, rammed by the *Stockholm* on that foggy midsummer night off Nantucket, just to make everything worse?

Her rescue from the listing ship, and her intuition that he'd shifted his attentions to Sophia, and then her venturing into the Treatment with Dr. Hartman, had seemed to change her. He didn't know what she'd become. And on top of that, Sophia had now run off and married Carlo Ponti, the Italian director who had discovered her when she was a teenager and hadn't let go. The Acrobat had begged her to abandon the married Ponti and marry him instead. He'd hardly felt guilty as he told Sophia how quickly he could divorce Betsy. Now he was in the bathroom, barricaded against foulmouthed insult.

Ear pressed on the door, he only registered silence from the other side. He turned the lock as softly as he could and slowly eased open the door. She was right there, sitting up in bed, as if nothing at all had happened.

"Are you quite done now?" he said.

"With our marriage?"

"With your profanity."

"I can't really say. Do you expect a wife who just endures it all, in silence?"

"I thought we were done with that regrettable interlude."

"Really? Interlude? I think we'd call it betrayal. I don't intend to serve as a placeholder, dear."

"I've never seen you this disrespectful."

"Yes, indeed I've spent years being the obedient wife. And how has that gone for me?"

He was standing at the foot of the bed, unsure how to answer.

"And do you know how painful, after all of that, to be left?" she said.

"I do, actually."

"You're obsessed with that damned girl, and now she's run off and gotten married. How bloody embarrassing for you!"

"I think you read too much into that, my dear."

"I saw it all on your face. It couldn't have been more legible."

"But as you said, she's gone off and gotten married now anyway."

Betsy seemed completely calm, sitting in bed, as if they were talking of small things.

"I stood on the deck of that ship," she said, "thinking about my sinking marriage. Then I got rescued. For this marriage of ours, I'm not going to wait for it all to sink."

"I suppose we'll need to take separate lifeboats, then," he finally said.

On Dr. Hartman's couch, he lay with his eyeshades in his hand, ready to take the dose. But when the doctor came in, the Acrobat said, "Before we start all this, I'd like to talk to you about what you're doing with my wife."

"We don't speak of other patients, you know that. Even when it's your wife. Even when she may not be your wife much longer."

"You know, I only decided to come here to find out what she was saying about me behind my back."

The doctor smiled. "The greater concern, I'd think, is what you've been hiding from yourself."

"Yes, that's why I actually showed up, I suppose. But I'm just so puzzled as to why this is all happening."

"That answer, I think, lies deep within," the doctor says, holding out the white dosage cup for him to receive. "Why don't we start, then?"

1959

AS THE TREATMENT ONCE again takes hold, on a sunny December Saturday afternoon shut out by the closed blinds, he's restless, on the couch, with the doctor close by. The new decade looms ever closer. Dr. Hartman will be the subject of a *Time* magazine article in the early months of 1960. But the American Medical Association is beginning to cast a wary eye. Rumors have begun swirling about certain governmental agencies using the medicine as torture, and some beatnik poets are beginning to give people the wrong ideas. And the Acrobat gets grayer at the edges, slightly more toward looking like the man in makeup back in January.

He feels the chill descend as the medicine announces itself, and maybe for that reason he's talkative.

"Would I sound foolish, Doctor, if I say that just as things threaten to be perfect, I'm aging too fast?"

"There's nothing we can do about that, other than mind our health and keep our minds lively."

"No doubt, at all. But I find I'm still obsessive about such small things."

"Maybe you haven't found the big thing you need."

"Still searching."

"Why have you never had children?"

"The thought terrifies me. I have no idea why."

"None of your wives have ever become pregnant? None of

your many girlfriends? None of your numerous conquests?"

"It is a mystery, I'll admit that. If anyone got pregnant, they certainly never told me."

"Some men consider numerous children a sign of their virility."

"I'm well aware. But I was raised by two people who had no idea how to look after a child, or possibly had no interest. Why do I think I'd do any better?"

"Maybe you'd do better for exactly that reason."

The Acrobat says no more. He's come to liken each treatment as a long flight through a high sky, and he knows he's only beginning to truly gain altitude. The doctor, as always, remains inscrutable.

This time, prompted perhaps, he has the most curious journey.

In it, he's in his tuxedo, as if in celebration, and he realizes he is walking down a long hallway. A door is at the very end. But he also realizes he is in his mother's womb, approaching his own birth. A journey beginning, but a journey ending as well.

Beyond the door, he can tell, are cold and blowing winds. But he feels heat under his clothing, as if under the glaring lights of a set. He admits to himself his fear. Through the door is life; through that door is pain. And confusion and elation and experience. And in life is the next door that is death, wherever that may lie.

And now the door gives way to a stage, and it opens to a parting curtain, and the applause and the warmth of an audience, and its love, and its anticipation. But he has no lines. Or he's forgotten them. He'll need to make it up as he goes.

Sunday morning, not in the familiar leather back couch of his own Rolls Silver Cloud, but in a less-obtrusive Lincoln he's arranged for Saturdays. Albert is behind the wheel, silent. Professional bearing, one might presume, or so many jobs carting big names that he hardly cares any longer.

The Acrobat is feeling a bit sunny, a bit sociable. Breakfast on his mind. He carefully chooses his cameos around Hollywood, well aware that sighting an elusive star is a lifetime thrill for some of the most devoted. For some of the less devoted, it's still notable. He remembers when he was first in town, how he saw William Powell, hot off *The Thin Man*, buying a sack of plums at the Grand Central Market. People around him looked without looking and traded sly glances. It had a powerful effect—a famous man buying plums—even as everyone acted as if nothing was happening at all.

Today it will be Canter's, on a morning in which the chill seems off-season. The deli runs twenty-four hours a day and late night is the busiest, but even early in the day the place is nearly full.

He's led to a booth and he duly plays his part, acting as if all eyes are not on him. Old Ben Canter, the owner, comes by with a solemn nod: Both are good for each other's business. He looks over the menu as a seen-'em-all waitress named Phyllis stands impatiently.

"Scrambled eggs and toast," he says, to Phyllis's stern countenance, above him as if carved of Rushmore granite. She grunts and is gone.

He wants to check the house, the way Bob Pender would peek through the heavy stage curtains before the troupe went on, counting bodies and converting it in his head to shillings. The Acrobat just wants to know he still holds his star power, and that there is no other person here who could divert that attention. But to look up would be to admit it. So he ponders his hands and waits for his coffee, which Phyllis quickly slides before him.

This act is akin to being a living statue, there to be considered and appreciated. He'll eat his breakfast as if in front of a lens, then recede as if this were not a performance. But his periphery has not been unguarded as he avoids eye contact, and he realizes somebody is sliding into his booth, onto the seat across from him. Two somebodies, in fact; a boy and a girl who look about eighteen or nineteen.

The Acrobat, well aware the imaginary camera is still rolling, smiles and says in his theater voice, "Well, I didn't know I had made a date."

An older woman across the aisle laughs from her booth, as if she's sitting in the movie theater, and he looks at her and gives her a wink before returning to his guests. The boy is in a striped T-shirt with a small beard capping his chin in the new style. The girl has pigtails in a child's style, and a turtleneck sweater.

"Hey, I know you from somewhere . . ." the boy says, grinning madly. "Like, somewhere, man . . ."

"I'm quite sure you have."

"Yeah, like somewhere from ancient history."

The girl giggles and the Acrobat says, "He is rather amusing, isn't he?"

"Yeah, man, you were like somebody, sometime, somewhere."

"Well, I was an actor, but I suppose now I'm a straw man."

"Like a scarecrow?"

The Acrobat grins tightly. "And was there something you two were here about?"

He can see Ben Canter, edging up but not sure what to make of it.

"Are you from the past?" the girl says.

"Past, present, future, dear. Take your pick."

"That's like, wow," the boy says. "I mean, you used to throw babies off the balcony, man."

The Acrobat stares for a just a second.

"I haven't the faintest . . ."

The girl says, "He means you used to be big."

"Six feet, two inches, just as always."

"Is that a joke?" the girl says.

"I'd like to think so. Do you want an autograph or something? What can I do for you two?"

They have no intention of leaving, it seems, but here comes Phyllis with his eggs and toast. She eyes the two kids in his booth and her eyes narrow.

"You two again? Didn't I already tell you to fuck off?"

Suddenly, they're scolded children, avoiding eye contact.

"Right now," Phyllis says, and they slide out of the booth. Phyllis motions to a very large young man, apparently a dishwasher, who has just been brought out of the kitchen.

"Juan, help these two find the door."

But the two don't fight it; the boy says, "You don't need to bring out the pearl diver, lady. We're gone."

They parade by mostly quizzical diners, and then are as quickly out on Fairfax, wandering.

"Beggars," Phyllis says to the Acrobat. "Druggies, I think. They bother people until someone gives them some money. They're probably going to go down to Schwartz's Bakery and bother the customers there. Then they take their drugs and start the whole thing all over again."

"It felt different than that. They didn't ask for money at all."

"You got me, then. Maybe you looked like an easy target . . ."

"I suppose the world as they know it is what they fight back at," he says.

In the back of a limousine, he's surveying what feels a fading empire. Abdication feels nearer than ever; the business he's known is largely gone, and the rules of the new game seem more puzzling.

But the force of habit is a tough thing to shake. The old saying is that an actor is retired when they stop casting you, but the illusions of the actor are many: Could you be the greatest old man in the history of the movies? Spencer Tracy was turning into such an elder; at fifty-nine he was starring in *The Old Man and the Sea* while the Acrobat, at fifty-five, just played a dashing young ad man.

But who had the heart to let yourself fall apart onscreen?

Now he sees Albert, his driver, looking at him through the rearview.

"Are you all right, sir?"

"Perfectly, Albert."

"Is there anything I can do, sir?"

"You're doing it, Albert, thank you."

And so they drive on in silence, the ending unclear, but the whisper of many possibilities up the road. But he's going home now, to the life he's built for himself, like a brilliant trick from the old stage, like a world made of light, like an image from a lens, conjured from nothing and made spectacular.

Tumbling

ALL THE WAY BACK *now, all the way to that dank kitchen with the fog outside the window and the coal burning so small in the hearth. That dark kitchen where the lamp's flame was dying and he was alone, and his mother was gone and he didn't know when his father would come through that door. Alone and frightened, desperate to be seen, to be heard, to be loved.*

All the way back to how invisible he felt, how untethered, how lost in the world. Back to the first stirrings of self-possession, the decision to move forward on his own. That moment is lost in his youth, maybe not such a decision as a slow recognition born of existential necessity. Dark days, with that small spark of ambition amid the ashes, and the larger urge for survival, and to enter the world.

And all the way forward now. The aging man. A life untouched by any war, by any economic calamity; a body untrammeled by disease; a career without downturn. The Lucky Man.

But it isn't over, either. He's got more traveling ahead, though he knows not where. Each morning the sun rises warm, and sets in a cobalt sky, as it will for millennia to come. But there will be that inevitable first morning where he is no longer alive to see it and the sun will shine without him. And that makes every sunrise until then a most precious thing.

And the vision now is of an old man with a child in his arms and the California sun lighting him as no spotlight ever did. Improbable as always, frightening and exciting. Time calling on him to finally play his true self. The Third Man, always waiting to be birthed, maybe now with the birth of a child. But he knows he's in his turns of the imagination, and in that of survival, above all things, that of hope.

And in his journey, he tumbles on.